The Dregs of the Day

The Dregs
of the Day

MÁIRTÍN Ó CADHAIN

TRANSLATED FROM THE IRISH BY ALAN TITLEY

YALE UNIVERSITY PRESS ■ NEW HAVEN & LONDON

A MARGELLOS
WORLD REPUBLIC OF LETTERS BOOK

The Margellos World Republic of Letters is dedicated to making literary works from around the globe available in English through translation. It brings to the English-speaking world the work of leading poets, novelists, essayists, philosophers, and playwrights from Europe, Latin America, Africa, Asia, and the Middle East to stimulate international discourse and creative exchange.

English-language copyright © 2019 by Cló Iar-Chonnacht.
Originally published in Irish as *Fuíoll Fuine*, Sáirséal & Dill, Dublin, 1970, copyright © Sáirséal & Dill/Cló Iar-Chonnacht, 1970/2019.

Yale University Press books may be purchased in quantity for educational, business, or promotional use. For information, please e-mail sales.press@yale.edu (U.S. office) or sales@yaleup.co.uk (U.K. office).

Set in Electra and Nobel types by Tseng Information Systems, Inc.
Printed in the United States of America.

Library of Congress Control Number: 2018966995
ISBN 978-0-300-24277-5 (paper : alk. paper)

A catalogue record for this book is available from the British Library.

This paper meets the requirements of ANSI/NISO z39.48-1992 (Permanence of Paper).

10 9 8 7 6 5 4 3 2 1

CONTENTS

This story, *The Dregs of the Day*, was the last published by Máirtín Ó Cadhain before his death. It appeared as the second part of a trilogy designed to mark a break from his earlier work. It can be described either as a novella or as a long short story, although writers are never too bothered about the minutiae of these genre wars. It was a story, like the best of his work, that began at the beginning and went on until its end, when its energy was spent, and it had spun itself out.

Máirtín Ó Cadhain (1906–1970) is recognized as the foremost author in Irish of the twentieth century, and one of the most talented prose writers of the country in his time. He is best known for his celebrated novel *Cré na Cille*, variously translated as *The Dirty Dust* or as *Graveyard Clay*. But it may be that he was better known in his lifetime as a writer of short stories, being the author of six collections, compared with two novels and a wild, anarchic prose work of indeterminate description entitled *Barbed Wire*.

He was born into an entirely Irish-speaking area of County Galway and said that he had never heard English spoken until he was six years of age. Because an understanding of Irish literature is often confined to those who have gained wide renown in

English, or indeed in French (in the case of Samuel Beckett), it is necessary to remind people that the Irish language was what was spoken by more or less all of the people of the island until the mid-seventeenth century, and was still that of the majority into and through much of the nineteenth. It would be crass, then, to suppose that the voluble Irish were silent for most of their history, and indeed, their deep prehistory. They weren't.

Most of what the Irish people ever said or spoke or uttered or dreamed or wondered or argued or made up was in the Irish language. Any disregard of this fact is cultural amnesia. After those yonks of expression in Irish, the language, like the people, was 'worsted in the game,' to quote Canon Sheehan. But it never got scrubbed out, and if that awful song 'Galway Bay' sometimes whined by visitors doesn't get murdered often enough, it contains the lines 'And the women in the uplands digging praties / speak a language that the strangers do not know.' It was a language known by the Irish themselves, quite often as the only tongue they spoke.

Ó Cadhain was one of those. Which means he inherited a rich literary and oral tradition, but one that was inevitably at some remove from what was going on in the rich fat cosmopolitan centres. He had no choice but to become acquainted in what is simplistically called 'modernism' as the waves of other thinking drowned his native shores. Coming from what is often dubbed a 'folk culture,' he transformed himself and his literature into the world of contemporary modern Europe, no matter how much that modern Europe is only a tiny isthmus of the bigger world.

It is often said that there were two Máirtín Ó Cadhains. The truth is, as with any great writer, there were many more. But this common division is an easy attempt to make distinct his early from his later work. His early stories were based on traditional Conamara life, using various techniques derived from the classical short story; his later stories could be urban, fantastic, experimental, parabolistic, or whatever. While not an entirely defensible distinction, it is a useful one.

This late novella needs to be put into perspective against his other work. His first published book was a translation into Irish of a bad novel by Charles J. Kickham, although in mitigation, it has to be said that all novels by Kickham were seriously bad. It must have been that he chose it because it was popular among country folk who knew no better and who supposed that because it dealt with the peasantry it had to be *ipso facto* of some worth. It is also possible that Ó Cadhain chose it because Kickham was a Fenian involved with radical, or just reasonable, national politics in the nineteenth century. This bad novel, *Sally Kavanagh*, dealt with the evils of landlordism and the tragedy of emigration, twin curses of Ireland that Ó Cadhain saw himself in his own place. He has often been described as a writer *engagé*, which he certainly was, but his stories were never propaganda and his literary writings never made you feel that he was hammering a political point home. He laid before readers what had to be exposed, then left them to draw their own conclusions.

The most salient point about his translation of *Sally Kavanagh* is, however, what he did with it. The version he was working from contained a little more than fifty thousand words; he returned to the publishers a manuscript of more than ninety thousand. This could hardly be called a faithful translation. From the start he showed himself to be a wordy smith.

This love affair with the wonder and the possibilities of the endless scope of language is central to all of his writing. In his case, it is the immersion in the creativity of the Irish language above all else that drives much of his style. This creativity is in stark contrast to the social and cultural situation in which his language found itself. This language in which it is written gives us one of the great literatures of the world and the longest unbroken vernacular tradition in Europe apart from Greek. Despite these glories that were not Rome but decidedly less barbaric, it found itself under assault and battery from the beginnings of the English conquest in the sixteenth century. The nobles abandoned it in the seventeenth, as nobles do; the urban outposts and the piddling middle classes in the eighteenth; in the nineteenth century the rural masses died from starvation or emigrated in their millions, leaving only the poorest of the most destitute speaking the language, mainly in the west of Ireland. Sometime during that century Ireland changed from being mainly Irish-speaking to mainly English-speaking.

Ó Cadhain was born into what he called himself, after Raymond Williams, a 'local organic community' in the *Gaeltacht*, or Irish-speaking area of Galway. He said that it was a community that had not changed in hundreds of years, and while this is not exactly true, the point he was making is easily understood. Life must have had a kind of timeless quality, the outside world was a glimmer illuminated only by rumours of what was out there, and by the occasional traveller who bent his tongue to bend the ears of his listeners. The only 'literature' was that of folk and wonder tales and local lore and whatever could be invented on the hoof. In other words, it was not unlike that of the 'unlettered' throughout most of rural Europe and the rest of the world.

For a young person bursting with imagination and creative energy this must have been confining, albeit he would not have known it at the time. Not surprisingly, his earliest stories, published in the collection *Idir Shúgradh is Dáiríre* (*Both mocking and serious*), have a folkish cut about them, and certainly do not give a hint that he had read much of modern literature apart from those dismal tales written by nineteenth-century Irish writers in English that even today are embarrassing to anti-postcolonialists. He never again speaks of these stories, and in a recent selection of his best, not one of these tales is included.

He tells us himself that his road to Damascus was picking up from a secondhand book barrow a French translation of a story by Maxim Gorki about a harvesting day on the banks of the Don. We have to imagine a roar of 'Eureka!' although maybe not exactly that word. He said, 'This is exactly what my own people do, this is their life, I never knew that this could be literature,' or words to that effect. He was making that connection with the wider world that would be a feature of the best of his writing from then on.

When he was interned by the Irish government during the

Second World War in what some people have described as a concentration camp—more accurately, an internment camp—he blossomed as a writer. It certainly concentrated his mind and creative energies. This was an unintended consequence, as the conditions in the camp were dire and savage and cold and bleak, as they were meant to be. But like many other political prisoners, he had the opportunity to read, to study, to talk, to debate, and he had the opportunity to write. We know from his letters written in prison that he read widely and copiously, and that this reading encompassed most of what passed for the contemporary literature available in Ireland at the time.

He wrote the short story 'The Road to Bright City' while he was a political prisoner. He tells us that this is the first story into which he put his heart and soul. He also tells us that it is loosely based on his mother, and on the lives of all those other mothers in the west of Ireland who had to save and slave and scrimp and sweat in order to earn the few miserly pence that might raise their family up, if only a smidgen. It is the story of a woman who gets up in the morning early before the cock even crows, to walk the long miles into the faraway city to sell eggs to garner a few pennies to make a little profit that will tide her family over until the next time around. Every turn and twist and hillock and hump of the journey is lovingly described, as well as the early morning traffickers who pass ghostly by; but the point of the story is that it dawns on her, even after the dawn itself breaks, that this is the life she is going to have to live forever. This is it, this is how it is going to be from now to eternity.

The classic short story often turns on such an epiphany. Ó Cadhain wrote some like that. They give us that moment of illumination that reveals the rest of someone's life; more often than not, this illumination is dark and pessimistic, or at least without the possibility of much joy.

Thus 'The Hare-Lip' tells us of a young bride who has been married by arrangement to a prosperous farmer in the fat lands of east Galway, in contradistinction to her own area of stony grey soil and meagre pickings. There is no suggestion that she is unhappy with the man she has been arranged to marry, or with the fine fresh fields she can look out upon. The story takes place during and after the fun and games that followed the wedding, and bit by bit, and one by one, and bye the bye she bids farewell to all those who have attended the ceremony. It appears, however, that she was always in love with a boy from her own area who had a hare lip, and when eventually all the guests depart, she looks at her own new husband snoozing at the fireside before they go to bed. He is fine, as it goes, but the one thing he doesn't have is that singular hare lip that the young man she fancied bore as a mark of distinction. Before her then stretch not only the fields and the far horizon, but a future that may be pleasant and more, but is most likely to be without love, without the magic she associated with her own place and with the man who had that beautiful distinctive hare lip.

Ó Cadhain has other stories like this, stories that go from description to dilemma to epiphany, not always happy. 'Floodtide,' for example, also brings us disillusionment, describing as it does just one morning in the life of a young newly married woman who has just returned from America to be with her promised sweetheart. Although life is still a honeymoon, she has to pitch in and help to harvest seaweed cooperatively from the unforgiving shore. She does her best despite the taunts and mockery of some neighbouring wenches who are more practiced than she in plucking seabeard from the rocks. Her husband is protective and defensive, covering up for her lack of practice while doing twice the work. It is only at the very end, when she fails to grab some of the more clingy seaweed from the rocks, that he shouts at her to get out of the way and let him do it. It is his harsh voice, the loud command, a tone she has never heard before, that shatters her romantic dream, and makes her realise that this hard graft and economic slavery is going to be the true story, not the dream she had dreamed in her dreams in New York.

I emphasise these stories, partly because of their unremitting realism, their depiction of life as it was lived in Irish Ireland without romanticism or mush, and partly because of their conforming to the traditional shape of the short story.

Those stories appeared in a collection entitled *The Dirty Drop* (*An Braon Broghach*). They were published before the novel which made him famous, *The Dirty Dust*. His next collection provided an even bleaker examination of the lives of women in an enclosed and often cruel society. Two of the stories in this collection, *Beside the Sea Shore* (*Cois Caoláire*), bear close attention. One of them tells of a woman who is unmarried and who sees her life without children ebbing away like the seepage that goes out of the bog next to where she is living. And while the symbolism is a bit obvious, the story is nevertheless powerful in its detail and unremittingness. In a similar fashion, another story with much the same precision and scary detail recounts the case of a woman whose children all either have died in childbirth or were stillborn, and who are buried in a local patch of land close to her own house. You feel that there is a burning rage at the harshness of fate within these stories, yet part of that fate is the circumstances in which the Irish-speaking rural poor have had to live.

These latter stories do not conform to the corset of the classical boring short story. Ó Cadhain was not a writer to be hemmed in by boundaries. The best of his work went on until it had said what it had to say, until its energy had been sapped, all breath spent, and then left it at that. He was constantly in search of a shape which would conform to the contours of his own imagination, and it may be, as for the best of writers, that he never found it. But he did claw away at it and discovered a form which was a wobbly frame and allowed him to wander. He parked this discovery for those years in which he remained silent as a writer and concentrated on his work as a university teacher.

His fame had been established by the publication of his novel *The Dirty Dust* in 1949. Novels always grab the attention of readers more than short stories because they create a wider world, presenting a life with scope and with context. Not every reader is attuned to the subtleties of the glancing epiphany and the nicey niceties of the buried symbol. Readers want a story up front in which they can participate with people like themselves and with concerns not dissimilar to their own. *The Dirty Dust* gave them this in spades and in shovels and in hoes and whatever else with which they dug. Its wider world is an entire re-creation of a complete community with all its beautiful loves and hates, its poisonous vicious spites and little generosities; it is more remarkable for the fact that all its characters are corpses in a local graveyard whose confinement does not in any way diminish their personality but rather enhances their humanity as people in a vivid time and place.

He wrote another novel, *Renewal* (*Athnuachan*), that had a similar structure and was entirely constructed of speech, but for legal and libelous reasons it was not published until a number of years after his death, and neither added to nor subtracted from his reputation.

After his release from prison in the years following the Second World War, Máirtín Ó Cadhain was banned from working as a schoolteacher because of his revolutionary politics. He spent some years working as a manual labourer, but mostly made a living by his writing and, for a short time, by working as a civil servant in the government translation service. This experience gave him ample material for some of his later stories, and elements of his disdain of the official mind can be found in this work. He also garnered some pennies by working as a part-time columnist for the *Irish Times*, a burden he abandoned when appointed as a lecturer in Irish in Trinity College, Dublin, in 1956.

This new position coincided with a long period without any

new published writings. This silence may have been because of the work involved in his new position—he was, after all, appointed to a university teaching position without the normal academic qualifications—or to a turn of his imagination that hungered after new forms, new themes, and new wonders. There is ample evidence that he took his new position extremely seriously and had little time for writing new stories; but there is also evidence that the wide reading he did in prison was voraciously added to in these barren writing years, and ultimately produced a different kind of writing in style and matter from what went before. Few writers can renew their craft and solemn art without knowing what is going on beyond themselves.

It is rarely useful to posit that an author has been influenced by him, her, or the other; and it is even more pointless to find a direct line of inspiration that can be specifically attributed. This academic detective game can never be proven and is generally bootless even to pursue. Still, when Ó Cadhain's next book of stories appeared in 1967, after fourteen years of silence, it was almost unrecognizable from his earlier work.

This collection of stories, *The Mown Swath* (*An tSraith ar Lár*), is a departure in almost every respect from his earlier work. A unifying theme of decay and resuscitation prevails—a theme that while present before, had never been so pronounced. The collection also contains what can best be described as prose poems and experimental writing in a wildly imaginative style. There are also parables, stories based on the Bible, and a long satirical story on the deathly hollows of the civil service.

More relevant, there are stories about his own *Gaeltacht*, his own place, which had been the locus for most of his earlier work. His own place has, however, been changed utterly. If it was ever a 'local organic community' — and it's doubtful if it ever was — it certainly isn't so now. The outside world has burst in upon it, the Irish language is riddled with Anglicisations, and people who still live the traditional life are left stranded in a world which is passing them by. Their tragedy is modernity, and modernity must be faced up to and dealt with.

This is where the easy critic begins to pick and to seek. Ó Cadhain himself never hid his admiration for Joyce; and his experimental prose has certainly gained inspiration from the wilder excesses of *Finnegans Wake*. Nor can there be any doubt that his beleaguered civil servant in *An Eochair* (*The key*) owes something to Kafka's single-lettered characters in *The Trial* and *The Castle*. While Kafka gives us K., and K. again, Ó Cadhain gives us J., the civil servant who becomes locked in an office over a weekend and who cannot be rescued because of red tape and regulations, and who eventually succumbs to hunger and to thirst. We might also see the hand of Karl Čapek's 'Apocryphal Tales' in some of his biblical short stories, particularly 'Riot' — but then again we might not, as Ó Cadhain read everything; and similarities abound in modern literature; and even if direct lines of connection could be established, all writers mash everything into their own imaginative sump, and the spider webs of inspiration will never entirely catch the flies of the critics.

In a television documentary made shortly after this collection was published and Ó Cadhain was back in the public eye, he said that he was then writing a book of stories that he hoped would be taken down from the shelf and read as long as the Irish language lived. This book was a sequel to *The Mown Swath* and was published in 1970, just months before he died. This story or novella, *The Dregs of the Day*, is the final piece in the collection.

On the surface it is a bleak story, but replete with pathos and sympathy for human frailty. The main character is another nameless cipher going through his wanderings under the letter N. He has just got news that his wife has died, and he goes into a kind of paralysis, which prevents him from dealing with the practical details of what has to be done. He is not necessarily a sympathetic person, but more or less a lost soul drifting along without compass or anchor, maybe a type of the uprooted blown about by the misfortunes of life. The simple psychologist (is there any other kind?) might have a fancy label for it that would make us all happy and make the difficult simple, the complicated plain, and the messy into the straightened lines of the reductive mind. But literature always darkens the horizon, deepens the colour, and wipes away the Grecian simplicities captured in a word with a suitably Hellenic root.

N. is none of these things. He is not forced to wander the earth like Cain, although his curse does seem to be that he will have no family, no home, nowhere to lay his head. He is not on a journey to anywhere seeking enlightenment, nor is he a seeker after wisdom, nor indeed the lonesome hero who comes over the hill to save something or other, especially himself. He is more like many of Beckett's characters, living in a world of confusion without either points of reference or lights of direction to guide his way.

In this manner Ó Cadhain has travelled countless miles and hundreds of years from his earlier stories, whose world was encompassed within certain definable limits. Those limits may well have been just the neighbour's patch, or the boundary wall, or what was heard beside a fireside, or the rumour from the bright city, or the expectation of the extra of little. Suddenly, and suddenly it was, the world was the locals' oyster and their *petite de fois gras* and their *Samundari Khazana* and their Matsutake mushrooms and their *Ayem Cemani* chicken, or whatever you are not having yourself. The outside world had come to Dublin, not just in the garb of outward appearances but in the innards of the internationally fashioned mind.

N. is buffeted by everything. In the first instance the shock of his wife's death; then his paralysed indecision, his disdain—to say the least—for his wife's sisters, his disengagement with his work colleagues, his cynicism about his job as a civil servant, his sense of uselessness as a television commentator, his meaningless entanglement with Squimzy, who was a good time had by many. There is always hope, but it comes in fits and starts, in the bookie's office betting on a horse, or in an engagement on a park bench, or a chance encounter on the street, or with his spiritual betters who should know, or even with a sailor whom he meets on the seashore and who offers him the traditional way out for all the disillusioned Irish. He is someone who cares, but who just doesn't know. He is, as in Beckett's famous phrase, someone who 'must go on,' because he has to go on, there is nothing else to do apart from to go on.

Indeed, one of Ó Cadhain's early traditional stories was entitled 'Going On.' It told of the desperation of the ordinary for whom life in poverty-stricken Irish-speaking Ireland—unlike those who lived in the lusher parts of the Anglicised east—was a never-ending struggle, neatly marrying two kinds of desperation: the one just of physical survival, the other for some kind of meaning or purpose. It may be that this is the story of the world: when you have learned how to go on, what is it that you do then with your going on once you have begun to go?

The Dregs of the Day is the story of an unravelling mind on the cusp of dissolution. It is a song of wandering anguish searching for something outside itself. In this sense, it is strangely religious. There is a savior out there somewhere, if only we could ascertain what or who it is. Yet the setting of the story, although in the rootless city, is determinedly Ireland in the 1960s. There are priests and nuns, and the Society of Vincent de Paul, and the Little Sisters of the Poor, and hostels to keep young women off the streets, people saying the rosary. Ó Cadhain did not realise, and could not have known, that all these things were going to fall apart within a few decades, and that the social face of the country would be changed forever. The fag-end of a certain kind of Catholic Ireland may give us much of the surface detail in the story, but N.'s desperation has nothing to do with this. It is of a different modern twist of sensibility.

Ó Cadhain was justifiably obsessed with the survival of his own Irish-speaking community. It drove his public life as an agitator and his literary life as a creative writer. *The Mown Swath* is a constant meditation on destruction and renewal. The first story, with the deceptively dull title 'The Old and the New,' encapsulates how that which was once revered and holy and worthy can be wiped away by the press of a button. It is no more than a detailed description of one Being hovering over another, the one Being a bomber, the other a city. It may be Hiroshima, or Nagasaki, or any other great metropolis wiped out just like that: 'Seven hundred years of growth, seven hundred years of work and sweat, of intelligence, seven hundred generations of love, of wisdom, of joy, all of it wiped out in unprecedented destruction, in a diseased swath laid low . . .' We have no doubt that this must be a symbol for the Irish language, for its literature, traditions, knowledge, wonders, and wisdom. It could hardly be a more explosive symbol.

Yet Máirtín Ó Cadhain was mostly concerned with the individual within that community—an individual with a dignity bound up with his own language—and just who he, or more often she, was. Thus his early stories depicted, without a smidgen of romanticism or a hint of the tear in the eye and the blather in the mouth, his own people as the wage slaves of history and the dogs of the poor.

As life changed he showed how those who didn't or wouldn't conform were dumped and shriveled and lessened as human beings, a process that would be smugly tabbed 'marginalised' today. The rich and privileged French intelligentsia invented what they called 'alienation' in a little roadside café called Les Deux Magots, which we might imagine referring to Jean-Paul Sartre and his sidekick, though she would have bristled at the characterisation, Simone de Beauvoir. They were among the most privileged of the superprivileged living a life in the centre of the establishment while pretending to be on the margins. It was one of the great con jobs of our time, taken up by the soft sofa sentiments of the most conservative student generation in history, who gave us in just a few years the exigencies of neoliberalism and the assaults of the next colonial wave.

Ó Cadhain just wanted to tell it as it was in his realistic stories. N. doesn't know what to do because all the traditional bets are off. There are hints of the olden power of the Catholic Church, of the borders between more sexual freedom and what used to be, of the call of the ever-powerful media, tempered by the pull of the local political Mafiosi, and of a life out there which just might happen to be realized. While the story is 'modernist' in mind and in style, the facts on the ground change. Apart from the fading of the Catholic dimension in our time—which to be fair had to be tied in with the arrangements for a funeral—we even have telephone boxes, those mysterious constructions which have to be explained to anybody of a certain age as you might explain the pyramids of Egypt.

The final stories in his trilogy on the theme of destruction and renewal, *The Swath Uplifted* (*An tSraith Tógtha*), had the appearance of the shavings of a leftover. You have to think that some of the efforts in this last book are drafts, and others are re-heatings of his earliest writings. It was certainly worth publish-ing, as most Irish speakers will say that everything he wrote is worth reading. It must be felt, however, that it was published as a conclusion to the trilogy which he had himself envisaged and planned, not because the stories therein—most likely just scrib-blings—approach the skill and imaginative daring of his two earlier collections in the series.

The Dregs of the Day stands at the conclusion of a long line of stories and novels which began with Ó Cadhain's apprentice-ship in the practice of translation in the 1920s; evolved into tales brilliantly written but inchoately folkloristic in the 1930s; be-came traditional in form and content in the 1940s, with the ex-ception of his great novel *The Dirty Dust*; developed in shape and depth in the 1950s; and culminated in an explosion of tales, anecdotes, parables, prose poems, yarns, stories, and novellas of the 1960s.

He was still learning to the end, as all writers do. This novella is modern and modernist, while bearing the marks of the 1960s and 1970s. But as with all literature there is that in it which be-longs to its time and place, and that which may be more univer-sal, whatever that means.

Most important of all, of course, it is a story. Stories are told in language, and unless you are tone blind and colour deaf, the way they are told is a great part of the reason why we engage at all with literature, as distinct from just the gabble in the street or the bland blank blabber of newspapers.

Ó Cadhain cut his literary fame from his command of language. He was once accused of packing every word in Irish from Barna to Carna, often seen as two borders of the Gaeltacht, into his great novel. These two rhyming place names weren't even half the story. He used every word and turn of phrase that just happened to be useful, as any writer in English will filch and purloin and turn and steal all that is out there in the language to describe what he, she, or they want to write. Ó Cadhain never saw local language as a prison in which he had to skulk. Any writer with an expansive imagination must needs let fly, or at least invent with all the tools that he can call on.

His early stories and his great novels were written in the speech of his own people, although infused with his own literary imagination. There is nothing in them that the alert reader of his own place and time will not readily grasp, any more than any reader wrestling with developed and enriching fiction in any language. He admitted, however, that he had spent most of his life in Dublin, and it would be wondrous strange if the urban landscape and mind were not expressed in his fiction.

On the surface, this might seem to be a problem. Although Irish had always been an urban language as well as a rural one, it had not been an urban literary language in any artistically wrought sense for several hundred years. The large Irish-speaking communities of Dublin, Belfast, Cork, and Galway had been done down and silenced in public discourse for a long time, and thus the depiction of an urban Irish-speaking population or coterie always appeared to be a difficulty for people of small brains.

The point about literature is, of course, the exercise of the imagination, and writers have scribbled about the past not knowing a puff of whatever language was spoken then, or about the future not even dreaming of what words might be uttered in the going-forward time beyond us all.

It wasn't the cityscape that presented the challenge, or just boring terminology, or even what we like to think of as the modern mind, which is not all that different from the mediaeval or the Cro-Magnon except that the prejudices of Fashionists have changed. It was that he was himself working constantly on new styles, turning the language over, weighing it differently, tasting it in a way in which it had never been chewed before, pulling and teasing the syntax to meet the demands of his own mind, inventing twists that might or not might work, being bold and inventive and risky. In this and in many other of his later stories he created a kind of Irish that was subtle, supple, stretched, and suitable, tentative, tough, thorough, and thought-through, but always inventive, imaginative, and innovating.

The translator will always have to deal with the problems that needed to be dealt with in his early stories. With his new style he can still lose control—sentences will go on until they run into the sand, a phrase will be followed until it is driven into its lair, words are invented or turned that find no easy equivalent. But this is how he wrote, and as with all writers, his greatest gift can be seen by others as his biggest weakness. There is nothing else he could ever have done.

Yet a story, for all its sociological impact, or its force for argument and example, must always be a story. This is a tale of a man at his most vulnerable, at his most confused, at his most lost, even lostest. There may or there may not be salvation out there. Who knows?

The Dregs of the Day

It was a ratty voice on the other end of the telephone, her sister calling from his house.

'Aren't you ashamed of yourself gallivanting around, and your wife just dead.'

'She is dead,' N. said. 'Yes.' It was as much as he could think of saying. With so many civil servants listening, he couldn't say that he had missed so much time in the office that his job was in danger. He had told her dozens of times that he had got lots of hints in the office already, but they wanted to believe that he was neglecting his wife . . .

'Dead at last,' he said, as he couldn't think of anything else to say.

'Yes, at last,' the sister said. 'You'd think it wasn't soon enough for you. Dead at last! Why don't you just get your ass home here? Everything has to be fixed up yet . . .'

The civil servants knew that she had died, and they gave him their condolences:

'You should have stayed at home today,' the Office Boss said. 'We're not that much behind with the crap. We could do with some job sharing, as we're one of the few offices open on a Saturday . . .'

'Advice for what it is worth,' N. said to himself as he went down the stairs. He wasn't thinking of the death, but of the funeral. She was to be buried. The preparation was some relief to him, the fact that things had to be done. He might manage to evade the attention of the two sisters for a while, escape from the constant poisonous peering that was always poring through him. Simon was great at this kind of stuff. He'd be able to get him a cut on the coffin and the grave. That's the kind of guy Simon was. He had the right contacts. N. gave him a buzz on the phone. Certainly: you'd think that Simon was thrilled that somebody had died: he could do something for his pals. He arranged to meet him in the Kitch Inn.

While N. was waiting for him he called an undertaker's who hadn't a clue who he was. When Simon told him the discount he would get in Lonergan's, N. knew full well that a coffin cost more there than in the joint he was talking to. And yea, yea, Simon went on about oak and ornamentations and goldy bits and pieces. Went on a bit too much, maybe. It dawned on N. quickly that maybe Simon would make his own bit out of the deal, and he let it go without making any real decision. Simon was waiting for two more telephone calls—he was, after all, a busy man— and N. used this as an excuse to head off, and he didn't tell him anything about where he was going. He didn't know himself . . .

They'd need a couple of bottles of whiskey. The sisters might want him to splash out more than that. After all, it was the end of the week, and the weather was great, and people would have gone away for the weekend. Nobody would know nothing much until it was too late to visit the house. It would be much cheaper to get the booze at Murphy's off-licence. If what Tom said was true he could get it at one pound eighteen and six pence, but Simon said half of it was Murphy's old piss anyway. N. had an idea where Tom was on Saturday. As luck would have it he caught up with him toddling down the street on his way to the Grain of Wheat. Tom had his own ways, you might say. He was a thorough gentleman, down to his fingertips. He said, the way things were, like, they'd only have one drink. They were already on the third, and Tom was only having them on . . .

N. remembered that his wife wouldn't have been laid out yet at home. Tom asked somebody in the pub that N. didn't know. He said something about a nurse who worked in the vicinity and suggested that N. call her. On his way to the telephone it dawned on N. that he didn't have the least clue from Adam who this guy was, nor did this guy have the smallest clue from Eve who he was either. He thought it a bit weird that some guy who didn't know who he was kept going on about the nurse. Then he thought of something else. The Little Sisters of the Poor would do this for feck all. The ugly sisters would be livid. What they wanted was a fancy regular nurse who would have a bag of tricks that she never opened, and a handbag as big as herself. There was a whiff of the beggar from the Little Sisters. That's what they said when he thought to ask them to come and look after his wife and to give him more time to go to work. But if two of the Sisters came in, it would be very difficult to shag them out again . . .

N. knew that the whole lot would cost a bomb. Tea, sugar,

guzzling, and gorging: that in itself would be massive, but it would only be the thin end of the wad. The sisters would organize the rest despite himself. And there was no way they would leave themselves behind the door. He imagined the huge fishgob of the older one sinking her snout into the cake he ordered specially for her. They didn't really give a toss how he would get on after this—he could be alive or dead for all they cared—just that their own sister was dead . . .

N. paused in the corridor. So it would go: the sisters would divide up and share out his wife's clothes and shoes and whatever else. He would certainly have a cause to crib from now on: and he needed every cent to live on. His tax allowance would be much reduced, if not completely gone. But he remembered that a dead person's possessions, especially a dead woman's possessions, would be given to the poor, to the beggars on the streets. And he also heard that the Salvation Army bought stuff like that and paid top dollar for it. If only they'd turn up, without even asking them! He knew full well what the old bitches her sisters would say: 'Christ wasn't dead in his grave and they were casting lots for his clothes . . .' But, hey, if this problem was urgent, if what had to be done had to be done, it was better if it were done quickly.

There was some guy in the telephone box ahead of him. N. arsed around for a while, but it didn't seem that your man was going to finish very soon. He had to buy another drink for Tom who was half with them, and half with some other gabbling gang. In order to avoid getting another drink for Larry, he copped on to head for the phone again. The man was gone, the Little Sisters of the Poor's phone was engaged, and there wasn't a bleep from the Salvation Army. Maybe they didn't work on a Saturday . . .

It was just then he thought of the church and the priest. There was so much to be done. It was one long loop and every ready palm had to be greased with money. Larry was the guy he depended on for this. He collected money for the church in the parish. He hadn't been rumbled yet with his hand in the till, unlike some others. He'd have a quiet word yet in the sacristan's ear as well as whatever the Holy Spirit might advise him to do. He'd tell the priest that N. was a poor man, that his wife was depending on whatever help she could get as he already knew, and because of her long illness that N. would have a lot more to put up with apart from the burial itself. Certainly, the priest would soften up a bit, he would have to . . .

Then N. clanked up another link in the chain. Wouldn't it be better to bring her to the church this very evening? That in itself would stymie much gorging and guzzling in the house. The ugly sisters would bring up the immediate necessity of the burial, and was it in the end any different from burying a dead mouse? It wasn't she who had to live any more but he himself, and if he had to live at all he had better have a few pence stashed away in his pocket. Things had to hurry up. The telephone was hammering away in the background all the time.

Larry had no memory of N. while he was outside. He was going on about the visit he paid that morning to the iron mongers' shop in Prickke Street:

'He's holding on to the typewriter he was keeping for you, N. It's as good as new. He said there were a few guys who wanted to buy it . . . But, hang on now, you're not really bothered about a typewriter, are you . . . ?'

N. didn't really know what was bugging him, or how much precisely he was worried. He was just overwhelmed by it all. Since the typewriter was hauled out of the lumber room of his memory, it would stay there pricking him like a boil on his hand, or an injured foot that wouldn't heal. N. did a bit of work off and on for the radio and for the TV. The typed word had a *cachet*, as they said in the office, that the handwritten scribble never had. When N. saw the fine fancy print on documents from the radio and from the government, he imagined that a handwritten script was like an unmarried woman. He had been jotting notes on a sheet of paper for a TV commentary which an official version was smothering with jargon when the news of her death came that morning. The news just about left space for one other thing in his head: that he was contracted to head off down to the midlands with Colm and his TV crew that very afternoon.

He had promised this a few months ago. They rang him yesterday to remind him. How could he know that that was the day of all days that his wife would die? He would have to go to the church early enough this evening. The TV crowd couldn't get a replacement just like that. If he let them down now without any notice he'd never get a stroke of work from them again. All he had to do was to call Micko in the office and he'd take over from him straight away, no problem. But the same Micko was waiting his chance to take over from him, whenever! There'd be no point in forgoing the money. He'd need it more than ever now. It certainly wouldn't do her any good, this day of all days, not to grab the chance. The worst thing he could do was to be arseing around the house. That's what her lot was best at, of course. It wasn't enough that today they would be down on him twice as badly as usual; and what was spent on booze and goodies would double their satisfaction. He told the rest of them that he had to send an urgent message, something not unusual for a body who had to look after a corpse.

When he left the place, it looked like he wouldn't delay further until everything was done and fixed up. When he was outside the door, however, he didn't turn right or left, neither this way nor that. What he had to do wasn't even vaguely in his mind. The road laid out before him was like a knife through the story of his life, dividing completely the past from the present. A melancholy maudlinness took hold of that part of him that might have helped him to take pity on himself. He might have stayed that way only that a cart loaded with trash furniture and other junk rattled into the street. N. remembered the huckster's shop and he toddled up along towards Prickke Street.

He almost clobbered the widow Waddel as she clattered out of the supermarket laid down with a veritable Croagh Patrick of groceries and goods. She was so taken up with the bargains she had grabbed she clean forgot to ask about his wife:

'The bargains, N.! Talk about a bargain! Do you see that pig's head?' She shaved back a sliver of the brown paper to show a

chunk of skull that a fly landed on immediately, readying itself
to start sucking the dried-up blood.

'It will do the business for a week, N.! Do you know what N.,
you'd get a full whack of dinner in there for as little as eighteen
pence?! You wouldn't mind, but think of the cost of the clothes
and the shoes and everything else!' It almost rose up into N.'s
mouth to ask her did she have a typewriter.

'It really pissed me off that I had to forget about the sales,
and those other bargains, but hey, N., that's how it goes. There's
always Monday and Tuesday with the help of God. A poor widow
has to . . .'

N. headed off until he felt sure that the widow Waddel was
gone. Then he turned on his heel and went in the door. He didn't
believe from what she had said that there would be so many
people in the department store. It wasn't that they were hauled in
like in a chain gang: he copped on that where most of the crowd
was gathered was precisely where the best bargains could be had.
He remembered some priest from the altar rattling on against
people looking for bargains. The seller deserved every last blood
penny he could get. Somehow, you'd know the department store
wasn't the word of God. There was a smartass in the office who
pretended that he read only learned books: 'N. goes shopping,'
he said one day, 'just the same way as he goes to the shit house,
so that people will know he was there, without leaving a plop
behind him. That was the reason N. only had shit thoughts. He
hadn't shat enough when he was a youngfella. He'd made a big
deal of having a shite . . .'

N. didn't agree with that at all, naturally, but unbeknownst to himself, and almost despite himself when he became aware of it, he loosened the clasp on his wallet. The small change first, and then the big dollops started appearing tentatively at first, and then pouring forth. Goods and goodies! Grabbing at whatever he could! Old dirty shirts which they only wanted somebody to shag off with without asking. The last pair of those shoes in the place! A Hoover going for nothing! A heater! If he wanted to, he could shave off another nail paring of the price from the boy behind the counter! But then, no matter how great a bargain it was, he could do with one a bit smaller, one just a bit more handy. Look at that! He hadn't gone near the Little Sisters yet, nor ordered a coffin, nor made any arrangements about the church, and yet there were at least two people, or maybe more, waiting for the host of the show!

The heater was like a whore's pimp standing out from the crowd. It had the same unhealthy but flashy look. But so what? He'd need the heat. Who'd set the fire from now on? In the sitting room, in the bedroom, maybe there were fires that would be never lit again? The house would freeze over without any heat. He loosened the strings of his purse, the flaps of his wallet. He screwed up his eyes as if he was looking through the eye of a needle in front of him. He put the small change and the larger amounts of money in his trouser pocket as they would be easier to get at. At the same time, he separated out a few notes from the rest as carefully and as solemnly as if he had been handed some precious secret that he was afraid to approach without due dignity. He knew every single note he had. He'd know them even by rubbing his finger against them. He knew full well how many he had. He had the funeral money ready and waiting. He hadn't spent any of it since the doctor told him finally, and twice, and again, that she wouldn't last too long more. He made sure that last time he had enough. He had enough. He had enough now for the bad times. He knew now that the expense wouldn't be as bad as he thought. There'd be no harm in putting a small hole in it. He wouldn't pass the heater up even though it wasn't slashed down as much as the Hoover. He had his wallet out again, opening it. That was precisely when the little whippersnapper dashed in, grabbed it more or less out of his grasp, and vanished as quickly as an eel between two rocks . . . N. started to scream. A crowd gathered around him in a flash stopping him from chasing after the robber.

Anybody with a bit of cop on would know that that wasn't the end of the story. He wasn't as shocked as you'd think. He gulped a bit and started to whine with self-pity. Did that young-fella, that robber, did he know that it was for his wife's funeral, that she had died only today? God save us all! Everyone down on the weak and helpless! May God look down on the poor woman laid out at home! It was worse for those who were left behind. That's how it was . . .

'The nasty little crook, your wallet swiped.' A woman who put her arm in his brought him back to his senses. He thought by the way her hand was shaking that she was rummaging around trying to find out did he have another wallet worth filching after the robber was gone. People were shouting out about the wallet, but it was hard to differentiate N.'s wallet from the general clamour about wallets and purses, 'my wallet, no my wallet, Daddy it's my wallet,' or 'murder,' or 'rape,' or any of the other screams that had little to do with the snatching of N.'s own wallet. After a while the shouts subsided, and N.'s wallet was the only one left to tickle the ears of those around who were by now getting a bit tired of the same old patter.

N. was hoping—still a likely hope—that the thief hadn't left the area yet, as the crowds were packed in and milling around.

'So, your wallet is stolen,' the manager said in a rough voice, obviously pissed off that he had to pay a bit of attention to this ordinary occurrence instead of taking care of the high-class moll who was fondling the heater. 'You should have taken better care of it.'

About twenty people whipped the words out of N.'s mouth:

'If nobody took out their wallets, Mister, nor women their purses, but kept them tightly under wraps in their oxter, then your lovely emporium wouldn't last too long, would it?'

'What are you on about? Do you think I should take out insurance on everybody's wallet and purse!'

The police had arrived and cordoned off the area before N. realized what was going on. N. had never seen in any office he had been in the likes of the notebook that the superintendent took out. He scribbled down N.'s name and address as well as the value of the wallet, its make, material, colour, folds, and clasp, if any. Just to hurry on this part of the investigation he took out his own and asked N. did it look anything like his. Then he asked some of the other police to do the same thing. Then wallets began to appear from all over the place like beetles on a floor. 'If all these wallets had been out a few minutes ago,' N. said, 'then there's no way mine would have been the one to be robbed!'

The superintendent started on another line of questioning. What time did N. come to the shop? How long was he there? Who did he speak to? Was he certain he had the wallet with him?—N.'s eyes widened as an answer to that particular question. At what precise time did he realize that the wallet was not in his possession? Then: What kind of a person stole the wallet? Young or old? Tall or small? Black or blond? Did he have a birthmark on his right cheek? Missing a front tooth? . . .

N. was beginning to get interested in these events in themselves. An image had appeared in his mind, a birthmark, a front tooth, a cauliflower ear, a scar under his jaw down to the collar of his shirt . . . That's exactly what a thief would look like. He began to think of him as someone who enjoyed snatching wallets and secreting them away without bothering to assess what was in them might be worth. Didn't people collect books, stamps, any old junk? Why wouldn't there be people who collected wallets just for their own sake, without a thought of profit? He wasn't mindful now as to the reason for the immediate executive cause of his own loss. Then his features faded away as it were, he appeared just like everyone else, a standard face unrecognizable from a hundred other faces in the shop with only one human saving grace left to it, which was this robbery in that particular shop. N. imagined serried ranks of shelves, thousands of wallets of every colour, every size and shape laid out in systematic series, every single one of them tagged as to where they were pilfered or purloined or swiped or snatched . . .

It would be difficult to assess how much longer N. could have been imagining this collection which his own wallet was helping to complete. But the super was looking for more details all the time. How come he had so much money? It wasn't that it was that much, but at the same time a lot for some guy to be hauling around in his pocket. N. thought he should ask him did he think he had robbed it himself. You'd never know, however, if a chancer like him had friends in high places. On the radio, maybe on television. Who did N. talk to since he left the office? How much brew had he consumed? Was he in the jacks? Did he take it out in the jacks to count it? Did the super really believe, even as a joke, that N. went to the jacks in order to count his money, or did he think that saving money had something to do with the other functions of going to the jacks, apart from the principal, main, legitimate ones? Did N. take it out when he was paying for a drink in the pub? If he took it out here in the department store how did he know he put it back? But N. said he didn't. It was swiped right here in the department store, and that was the last time he had taken it out. He swore black and blue, again and again, that the wallet was robbed right here, in this here shop. It appeared that the super was reluctant to admit even that much . . .

N. sometimes thought of writing his life story. But he often admitted to himself that his story wasn't worth telling. He had spent most of it messing around with insignificant details, with dross, with the flies that attach themselves to the big wheel of fortune, he told himself. But the questioning set his mind whirring again. It seemed to him that his life was beginning right now. How would you get a startling opening better than being robbed? The stories he read started to tumble around in his head. He couldn't actually remember a story which started with a robbery, not to mention a robbery on exactly the same day his wife died. He'd have to be discreet about it, and keep his gob shut!

'That'll do for now,' the super said.

N. suddenly thought about his situation: 'Has my wallet been found?' he asked.

'The Gardaí are still questioning and searching people around and about,' the super said. 'People who are known to us. We'll get on to them at home. Be thankful if we get them.'

That last phrase frightened the shite out of him more than anything else that had been said since his wallet was stolen. It awoke him from the romantic slush of the imagination to the hard reality of the shop and the cruel grasp of commerce, not to mention agreements, wills, burials, and all the bitchiness that was waiting for him at home.

N. never remembered losing anything worthwhile apart from a pair of gloves he left on a bus. Even after he went to the Lost Property Office they were never found. Wouldn't a wallet be worth much more than that? Suppose the thief took fright and dumped it on the floor? Wouldn't it have been easier for some other bod to stuff it in his pocket, somebody who was hanging around, somebody who was not known to the Gardaí? Why suppose that anyone was as nice, so to speak, as his best friend, Simon? If Simon was making a crust on coffins and graves, on deaths and debts, on his friend's misfortune, wouldn't he keep his wallet as well? How long would it take him to hive off a bit on a coffin or a grave compared with what he would get on a single wallet, like N.'s.? Wouldn't others do just the same? The manager of the department store, for example? He might spot it on the floor, maybe, and slip it under the counter with his foot so that it would be his when everyone else had cleared off. Why wouldn't he? His job was robbing people, wasn't it? And if the manager could do it, why couldn't the cop? He'd be brilliant at it, unfortunately! N. thought that the super had delayed things deliberately, so the Gardaí would have a chance to filch the thing themselves. He often heard that the cops claimed anything that came their way. Even if they found his wallet, how many hands would it pass through between the robber and himself? Even the cop who found it wouldn't pass it on without taking his own pound of flesh from it, that's if the robber had left anything in it at all. Wouldn't it be easy to lay all the blame on the thief? And every Garda and fuzz and pig up all the way to the top!

And then there were expenses. It would be a fairly-gutted wallet by the time it reached N. It might be just as well to let bygones be bygones now and forget about it. N. was still angry that he was getting no joy it didn't matter where he turned. But he fucked the widow Waddel and her bargains from a height, a good clean fuck. He knew that he would never have met her if it wasn't for the one who sent her to the secondhand junk shop and dumped the whole story on him. And he thought that if it wasn't for his wife dying he would never have fallen into her clutches. She died at a messy time, death is always messy, God help us all, N. said.

N. was feeling sorry for himself until he ended up in the department store and feeling sorry for the woman who had died at home; except then again, he thought that the living deserved more pity than the dead, who couldn't feel it any more either. But he didn't let the wallet completely slink out of his mind. He still had a weird expectation of getting it back. He had heard of sums of money that had been recovered in the most unlikely ways. God in his goodness wouldn't let everybody leave the department store without some kind person finding it in an unexpected place . . .

He mingled in around the crowds not taking much notice of himself or of anybody else. Nobody could steal nothing from him now. Even if they found his wallet this late in the day, it would have been no thanks to him. He had to keep moving. He was bumping into people and jostling them. He stamped the flat of his own foot down on an old woman's trotters. They called her type a 'Logogeographer' in the office, because of the way she could place her words. She called him all the shitty names she could think of from the map of Ireland and every other shitty name from every shitty hole in her own shitty body. Small things like this kept him on the straight and narrow between the looming trough of despond and the impossible veil of the unknown future. The manager would never believe he was just being stubborn. N. never really took any notice of his voice until he spoke roughly, even sharply. 'Don't you hear me? I'm talking to you for the last half an hour. Can't you see that people are leaving the shop because of you? Why don't you feck off home with you now and as soon as the Gardaí have any news they will let you know.'

The manager wanted to get rid of him. He squeezed his nails into his arm until they hurt. The peace and quiet of the street whelmed him as somebody who hardly deserved it, as somebody who had more than enough to do, going in as he did and coming out like a lousy beggar. The streets were as empty as his own pockets. There wouldn't be a soul around if it wasn't for the department store. There was neither music, nor noise, nor traffic to divert his attention. He took out his hankie to wipe his forehead. He determined to banish the remains of all those sweaty breaths from himself.

He sat down on a seat on his own by the side of the street. The thing he had to deal with was much thornier than just the business of the coffin and the grave, something else that had to be dealt with before all else: what would he do about his wallet, with the fact that he simply had no money? This was a hard question, but actually quite straightforward also. His wife was not going to live. Therefore, it followed there had to be a coffin and a grave. But the theft of his wallet was a blow, a savage blow, a defining blow. His wallet was part of the furniture. He couldn't imagine anything in his life without it. It was as intimate a part of him as anything else. Maybe it was no more than that it was a great comfort there under your oxter, like the hand of a lover under your arm and around your heart. And when you'd feel it there in the shop it was a comfort for your hand, or for the spring in your step, or the glint in your eye, a kind of defense for the whole personality, like a royal seal of approval on your spirit! N. remembered reading something like that when he was researching stuff for a radio programme. Certainly, in that case, you would speak louder, and more clearly, and with greater certainty, and even in a fancy voice. You wouldn't even have to buy anything. It was enough to ask for something but to make certain that they knew you had the means. N. stuck his left hand in under his arm. Nothing there. Oh, my God, 'Nothing between today and yesterday: less than to keep death itself at bay?' It was natural for death to come. But God didn't ordain that a wallet would be stolen. 'Holy Mary, mother of God! God save us from all harm . . .'

'What's this you're on about? What did you say about small farmers? Wake up. You're pissed blotto this early in the day? . . .'

N. didn't know how long this other one was plonked on the same seat, a big blubbering buffoon whose clothes might have belonged to a Christian Brother once upon a time and who wasn't short of advice for N. It didn't take him long to winkle out the bit about his wife's death and the stolen wallet.

'Now then,' he said, straightening himself up in such a way that you'd imagine that being straight was his normal bearing. 'Take my advice to heart, I'm telling you. This here isn't a place for messing around or for hanging about, seeing as that your wife isn't buried yet. I wouldn't have dreamt sitting down here on this seat only that I spotted you, took pity on you, and thought it would be an act of charity to give you some advice. It's no excuse that your wallet has been stolen. It'll be a while before they solve that. Don't let lack of money stop you buying or ordering anything. You'll pay them alright, you'll see to it. Nobody pays for a funeral and everything to do with it, the coffin and the grave and so on, until it is all over. Nobody is going to ask a man whose wife has just died has he got his wallet ready or not. Keep your trap shut about it all. Don't drink another drop. Go on home. Get a nurse to look after the corpse. Organise the grave, the coffin . . .'

N. was about to ask him did he know anybody who could get him a discount, but then the truth of the man's words swept through him as sharp, cold, and uncomfortable as a blast of snow that had slapped him in the face. He promised him he'd go on home straight away.

Just up beyond the arch, where a lot of people were moving, there was a nun with a box collecting money. Without glancing once in her direction, N. avoided her on the other side of the pavement as far as he could. He always did that. He couldn't even begin to explain to the nun why he had no money. She'd hardly worry her wimple the slightest about such a fantastic story, and if she did she would twist it to her own ends.

He took his time looking at offers of discount in McCabe's big window. He was hardly reading them, or even seeing them. He was trying to work out what he should do. He was asking himself what the fuck he should do. He promised the big blubbery bollocks that he was going straight home. But was he? This was certainly the way home. But it was also the way to a lot of other places. Did he really think, when he left the meddling buffoon, did he really think he would take another path, another direction rather than just going straight home? Where else would he be going except going home? He had to go home. Had he ever thought, now or ever, that he wasn't going to go home? . . .

It was then that he got a hearty slap on the shoulder. It was the guy they called Horse, his mouth stuffed up with that hope which was the overture of the gambler:

'I'm off home to get more money. I haven't enough on me . . . The man who hasn't enough money, he should rob a bank or something . . . My house and all on Trotterine! I spent all of last night with a man from the Standing Stud. And I spent the rest of the night dreaming that there I was there at the winning post and Trotterine flying past ten lengths ahead of everyone else . . . Isn't that a sign if ever you wanted one? She was eleven to one in the paper this morning but she's only five to one now, the latest odds. Look, she won . . .'

In four or five sweeping poetic equine sentences the Horse described briefly, but without hesitating, Trotterine's big wins during the last year. N. kept looking after him until the trail of his coat vanished around the corner just as a horse's tail would vanish around the corner of a racecourse. To N. meeting the Horse was like a life buoy thrown to a drowning man. He felt he should follow him, should stay inside the shelter of his hope and his confidence . . .

There was a crowd in the bookie's. They had gathered there without the slightest hesitation or doubt in their bearing, the shaft of sun from across the street striking a pose on the tops of their coats. He heard the race being discussed, things being said and sworn with such solemnity that you'd think they were the whole truth and nothing but the truth. The air was stifling. If fate was to visit him here, it would certainly come riding on the back of Trotterine! N. was fingering a half a crown in his pocket. He walked in and placed the bet. Even better than that, he'd wager a pound as he had heard that Trotterine's chances had soared. It would be something for nothing, although he'd still be a long time getting back what he had lost. The odds had shortened again. People were talking about betting their whole week's wages, their shirts and all. N. could feel the itch tickling his fingers in his pocket. If she won, he'd never forgive himself for not having a go.

He took a pound, seven shillings, thirteen and six pence, coins and all out of his pocket. If he won, you couldn't say that one arm would be as long as the other going home. And he wouldn't be completely stony broke buying the stuff for the funeral. If he was too late to go to the church later that evening, the few extra pence in his pocket would give him the courage to say to the ugly sisters, 'Is there any need to get anything else now?' and then to blow off down the country with the television

crew without further ado. Those couple of hours were hardly a
gnat's nip out of the day. He kept back a half a crown and bet
eleven shillings. Then he allowed himself to sink into the crowd
of people who were more or less all of one will, one mind, one
desire, one life's hope. A sourpussed oul Biddy who had stringy
strands of grey hair sprouting out through her black mop kept
extolling Trotterine's many wins. She went on a bit, but N. didn't
really like the fact that her fat arse was tight against his hip; but
then again, her eulogies for Trotterine were music to his ears.
He'd put every single thing, even the corpse that was waiting for
him, out of his mind until Trotterine romped home. Wasn't it a
pity that he didn't turn up here this morning instead of heading
for the department store!

The crowd were huddled around a monitor from which the
race was being broadcast. 'She'll win . . . Up the yard . . . Good
on ya . . . She has to . . . It's in the bag . . . Come on ya good thing
. . . She'll do it yet . . .'

Good old Trotterine came in third. It didn't matter much to
N. that all that was left of the excited crowd, of whom he was one,
was a busted flush whose talk consisted of sighs and groans and
gobs of disgusted spittled glob upon the floor. N. felt worse about
losing that particular bet than if he had squandered all of his
money. It began to dawn on him that the purpose of the Horse
was first to tempt you in and then to fuck you up. Maybe, however, despite that, he had managed to get something from it all.
He said he had spent last night with someone from the Standing
Stud. Simon all the way!

When that particular fantasy had evaporated, he knew he couldn't put the business of the corpse off any longer. He hadn't contacted the Little Sisters yet. He thought about the nun he had spotted below at the arch just a while ago. He made his way back to see if he could get any information from her about the Little Sisters, or indeed, about anything else. He'd give her something. He still had a few shillings left. But there was neither a saint nor a sinner at the arch. He searched around the neighbouring streets—but in vain. Went into a little shop nearby. The shopkeeper knew something about what she was selling but knew nothing else about her. Most likely she was finished and had gone. The crowds who were around had usually dispersed by two o'clock on a Saturday.

Nothing else filled his mind more than the fact that he had to contact the Little Sisters. Better do it late than never or not at all. He'd go to the hotel where he had left Simon. He'd be pissing around there still. That's the kind of headbanger he was. He'd love to hear what Simon thought about what had happened to him now. When he'd hear about his loss he'd go all soft and friendly and get him a cut without thinking of anything for himself. He'd be totally fucked if . . .

There were two people talking at the door of the hotel.

'Take it easy there, my parched pard,' one of them said to N. who was trying to push through the door, 'not until half past three. Did you get on a lucky one with the horses, or what? If you did—'

But N. had already slinked off. He got a sixpenny bit and

went into a telephone box. He immediately started scrabbling through the telephone book looking for the number of the Sisters. Then suddenly, the shock! It just couldn't be that he had fallen asleep! He was stunned. That particular page was not in the book. He thought of calling the exchange, but there was a sudden rattling on the door behind him. There were three young ones outside waiting and their impatience burned through him with the savage look in their eyes. N. pressed the button, the button that meant that his money clinked back all the way to the post office. Everything was going against him, just as if he was subjected to an ancient curse which stole money from his ancestors.

But maybe it was all for the best, anyway. It was getting too late to call the Sisters. The most likely thing now was that they'd come along when the corpse was already laid out. They'd think that N. was making an eejit of them. And what use would losing the head be, or pissing off her sisters any more. They'd have to make their own decisions and plough on in their own way, as they hadn't a notion where he was or how to contact him. The most reasonable thing now was to presume that the corpse was laid out appropriately.

If N. managed to make it home, he could fix things up one way or the other. He could say he was totally demented, the death of course, that he passed out on the way home, that he collapsed on the street, didn't know how long he was out for, was brought into a pub, given a brandy, which made him tipsy and fall asleep. With all the messing and the confusion his wallet was stolen, whether that was on the street or when he was conked out, he couldn't say. He'd have to tell them about the wallet. They'd be told anyway. It would be better if he was the first with the story. Everything was falling into place neatly. He'd nearly believe this bullshit himself! The sisters would say he was a dirty drunken sot! That he preferred to fill up his own boozy belly than come home and look after his wife's body. It didn't matter if he had a decent excuse or just a pack of lies, the sisters would flail him alive and have his guts for garters. But he still had to have some kind of an excuse. It was clear that an excuse was as much a necessity as anything else for the funeral . . .

This thought gave him such a lift that he imagined he was floating on air. His arms were light and as flighty as the wings of a bird, especially after offloading the iron chains which were weighing him down. He was almost hopping and skipping and jauncing his way home.

Even though he couldn't wait, he had to stop at the crossroads as the lights were against him. One of the cars that went by was a hearse with no coffin in it. It was so clean and snazzy from the driver inside to the fancy decorations on top that you'd think it came straight out of the car wash. It was probably scrubbed clean after every corpse was brought to its last resting place anyway. It made N. sad and morose just to see the hearse. He knew that it was just another branch of his misfortune to meet this particular junction on the road of the journey of his life at a bad time. If it wasn't for that he wouldn't have paid the hearse a blind bit of notice, and neither the coffin, nor the grave, nor the mourners, nor the burial would be looming up before him like an unsolvable problem . . .

He was heading off in a rush to see Simon a little while ago. Only God knew where Simon was—that is if God himself knew where people who were hell bent on destruction were hiding out. He could phone his house. But what good would that be? His wife would blame N. completely that he wasn't at home, totally blame him for all the times he wasn't at home or with his family. He was never there to recite the Rosary with them these previous six months. She almost said to N. the last time he phoned that it was his, that is N.'s, fault that she wasn't getting her rightful amount of the rumpy-pumpy. Was there anybody else he could talk to? Could he phone someone in the office? They'd all call each other back saying 'But I wouldn't like to . . .' and that N. was off the wagon and they were sure hoping that he wasn't going to fall down in front of someone at the funeral, especially now that one or two of the big boys from the Department of Domesticity were going to be there. Of course, his colleagues wouldn't say that N. was untrustworthy, nor that he could never be left in charge of any government business. That's exactly why they would call one another, just to remind themselves and make the picture clear. But it was now or never that he needed the money. He was well got with some of the radio and television gang, but maybe they'd take too much pity on him and he wouldn't get another stroke of work from them for a long time.

Just as he was going past a shop he spotted a man's face; it was as if it was laid out on the counter, a man's face, as kind a face as he ever had seen. Somebody with a face like that could only give good advice, helpful advice. Shopkeepers sold every kind of gadget, and their places were full of all kinds of junk, especially those small shops lurking in backstreets. He'd buy a box of matches and try to strike up a conversation. But instead of kindness he was met by a shock of surprise that surged from deep down, a shock that showed he never expected to be asked such a question inside the hallowed walls of his own place. This immediately turned into a kind of canny caution.

'Who the hell are you . . . Are you trying to rob me, or what? . . . There was a guy robbed in the department store the other day. Are you the robber? . . . Or worse than that. You're a whacko, a nutter! . . .'

A man he knew walked in through the door, and the shopkeeper resumed his normal placid mien, the mask he habitually wore for the public, presumably.

'Why did you leave it so long?' the newcomer asked N. 'You won't be able to get any burial now until Monday. You might just about get a coffin, but what use is that without somewhere to bury her? . . . Yes, I know, she has to be brought to the church. Even that much? . . . . It's quarter past three now. Did you say she has to be in the church at half past six at the latest? I'm not saying it can't be done. But you'll be put to the pin of your collar. Would they even take a body into any church until Monday? Who knows! Anyway, if you intend making a start, you should be off home pronto by now . . .'

The man guided him out. He gave him the name of an undertaker. After all the depressing talk that N. had heard already, the information slipped down into the garbage of his memory. A second later he wasn't even trying to retain it. But the man was becoming more sympathetic all the time.

'Here,' he said, taking him by the shoulder down a side street and leading him into a pub which was just opening again, 'a drink is a great help sometimes . . . He'll have a ball of malt to settle him, and give him enough courage to go home, where he should be.'

He explained N.'s situation to the barman.

'He's the thug who's swiping handbags from women around here,' the barman said, and he poured out another shot. The two of them told N. in no uncertain terms that this was not a time for messing around. He had to high tail it off straight home. The man showed him the nearest place to get a bus.

A new idea had just hatched in N.'s brain. Even if he wanted to, he couldn't put words on this frail flicker which had flashed in the embers of his mind. It wasn't really an idea, more of a feeling, a feeling that expressed itself more in his body than in his mind. He'd be better off hanging out with these two for another bit. That would be far preferable than hanging out with a corpse. A corpse was of no use, nor could it do any harm. His own corpse, that is, his own body was only waiting to be cast aside as a piece of useless junk, as unpleasant detritus and dangerous dregs. That is why people gathered around a corpse as long as it wasn't buried. There was really no communication between the living and the

dead. It was communication of a kind, but more like a man trying to read a book of blank pages. Good people when they were
alive could show humanity, charity, mercy, pity, and even Chris-
tianity. He had a fierce need for all of them right now. These two
were not a bit like Simon, nor the crowd in the office, nor especially the ugly sisters. If it wasn't for the likes of these life would
not be worth living. N. often heard it said that everyone knew
who the bad people were, but we never recognized all the good
people around us.

It was said that the Son of God could be working beside you
in the office or drinking down in the local hostelry and nobody
would cop on to who he was except someone who was holy. N. remembered only a short time ago that he heard a priest say that
if it wasn't for the good people on earth that God would have
scrubbed us out long ago, as he had done with Sodom and Go-
morrah. The bad person doesn't recognize the good person, but
all the good people recognize one another. N. heard Simon saying that a priest wouldn't know a good person if he jumped up
and hit him with sanctifying grace. 'But, of course,' he said cyni-
cally, 'isn't he making his living anyway from the bad people?'
'He knows the people who are in at the Rosary alright,' Larry said.
'When he was holding forth at the Rosary the other night, he
couldn't take his eyes from where Gorgeous Gulch had planked
herself down. Did I see you there too, or was I just imagining
it? . . .' Did that good person in the shop recognize that N. was
a good person too, did he? Not me, N. thought. He couldn't say
that he was a totally bad guy, of course. He'd never steal a wallet,

for one. Nor would he try to get a cut off the price of coffins, or funerals, or even a cheap bet on the horses. Nor did he ever try to do someone down in the office, or to block somebody going on the radio or the television. Whatever he had earned himself on radio or on television he had deserved it. He paid his debts and his taxes, but he hardly had any choice about the taxes anyway. Whatever else could he do in order to become a good person every inch of the way under God's blue sky? Stand drinks for everybody on the piss, whoever they were? That was an expensive business, and N. knew he could never do it again whatever about now. But maybe God had his own list of good people . . .

N. turned around to talk to the man about this new feeling he had. But he had vanished. N. remembered how Christ revealed himself to his disciples in the gospels sometimes, but then he would disappear just as quickly. But, of course, he also remembered that standing someone a drink who was thirsty was part of God's plan as well . . .

This good guy had squeezed a promise from N. that he would go straight home. Instead of getting the bus there and then by the side of the road, he decided to take a shortcut across the public park, where he'd get it for two pence less. Every penny had to be saved from now on. He wasn't really thinking of that either, but of all the old shortcuts in the city which were part of his legs and of his eyes for a long time. He would love to let some of the clean air, the clean, living breath of leaves and of trees, to kiss his body before it met up with a corpse that had no breath at all. It might cure him to listen and to understand prattle that had nothing whatever to do with him. He needed a breather before the battle. Her sisters would never shut their mouths until she was buried, and then he'd be able to banish their company from his life, along with the thumping of his heart and their ceaseless croneful clatter . . .

N. looked carefully at the side of the seat. He sat down and closed his eyes against the glare of the sun. There was a gentle heat in the day which made his head a bit dozy, just like it was before he invented the story about feeling faint. I might as well make use of it, the freebie, N. said, you'd get nothing else for nothing around here. He heard a clock strike, reminding him it must be four o' clock or later. The day has been stolen from me, just like my wallet, he said. Had he left everything far too late? His patience had long been exhausted by her sisters. They called their brother. He was a bad-mannered git, but he could be alright sometimes. He'd arrange everything and let N. pick up the tab. He would too! What was the first thing the brother would do? The sun was seeding the questions in N.'s head. Then he felt some of the questions he had thought of slip sliding away like the name of the undertaker just now. He tried to keep a hold of them as they had come to him, but despite himself they were falling away down a chute, down a chute into some black hole from which they could never be retrieved. He opened his eyes from this daze to see the bright panting puffs of breath of a woman just in front of him.

'I was asleep,' he said, and for some reason he could hardly take his eyes from hers, they were big tired eyes like the eyes of a fish, and almost as bulgingly bald too. The rest of her face was only so much *décor* for the eyes, the black circles like fly shit under her eyes, the obvious lumps of powder, too much war paint, the blazing red of her mouth. He imagined that those eyes stared out at him from the prehistoric muck, from the elemental mud, from the slob of slime.

'Forty winks of sleep would do you no harm, but not exactly here. Your money might get swiped in this place': her face lit up a bit, but N. wasn't sure was it a laugh or a grin or something else. If a fish's eyes ever laughed it would be just like that, the kind of laugh which had been determined for eons, a laugh which obviously followed the inevitable path of evolution.

'You were on the piss?' she said. But without giving him a chance to respond: 'You're tired out.'

Then, almost unthinkingly, like the most natural thing in the world, she lifted up her skirt above her shins to examine her foot.

'That's a nice piece of leg, especially if it was rubbing up against you,' N. said, never realizing that he was thinking out loud.

'Do you think so?' she asked.

For the first time a pleasant human smile burst upon the hardened iron lines which seemed like wires etched upon her brow.

'I do,' N. had to say. If he had got another chance, he wouldn't have said that. He imagined that this problem could have been easily solved in the beginning but was in danger of being entangled up, enmeshed and enmangled like the last one.

Why would he, N., be talking about a strange woman's big of leg in a public park as if a woman's leg was a kind or species of public property? And then on top of that, his wife laid out at home.

'You're really flayed out, you poor thing,' she said, and then the palm of her hand travelled with style until it rested on his knee, the one closest to herself.

'If you feel up to it, my own place is only across the road. You can cool it there. It might let you come to again, be up for it again. Who knows, we could have a drink after that?'

N. didn't refuse, as there weren't too many more offers. He'd be in off the street anyway. Most likely the ugly sisters would send out an emergency that he was missing. They were like that.

But N. wasn't happy yet to let things be. He still felt he should do something, anything, about what was happening at home. But he hadn't a clue what that might be. Nobody told him, neither saint nor sinner, good guy nor bad guy, what should be done. He had no idea how he managed to keep a grip on himself at precisely that time when he was about to reveal the misfortunes of his life and times to this here woman. But did he really know if it made sense to be talking to her at all, or sitting by her side on the park bench? N. said to himself that he didn't and decided to keep his distance straight away.

'I have urgent business to attend to.'

'But wouldn't it be better if you relaxed for a while first, scrub up a bit . . .'

'It's important, important business. Where will you be . . . around eight o'clock say? . . . Here. On this bench . . . I'll be here, for sure. A telephone call's no good. In that case the other crowd would try to discuss it on the telephone and I'd prefer to talk to them face to face. We're talking about a lot of money . . .'

N. was talking about his wallet. This chatter reminded him that the sooner he started to get his act together the quicker his torment would pass. He had to make that phone call. To the undertakers? The cemetery? The church? Home? Calling home was the easiest and probably for the best. But he couldn't call unless he could say that he had made some preparations, even if those preparations had been made by those already there.

N. had already reached the telephone box on the other side of the park. He cringed back from it as if it were a slimy worm ready to devour him. He sat down on a seat on the side of the pathway. He examined every one of the options he had before him. It didn't dawn on him that he had his two hands tied behind his back, and that it was all a matter of chance. When it came right down to it, did he have any choice? Was there really any question of choice in these matters? The whole thing was like a preordained chain of events, just like that woman's laugh, but he had no clue as to where the first link in the chain was, never mind the last. It seemed to him that bringing her to the church was the first thing to be arranged, but how could that be done without a coffin? And even if he had a coffin he'd still have to have an undertaker to take her to the church, and it was likely that no undertaker was available. But if it came to that, N. hadn't the least clue if a coffin or even a church was available. It was like trying to drink a blending of whiskey and water together and trying to tell one from the other. N. came to the same conclusion from this simple reasoning: it was too late. It was far easier to suppose — whether it was right or wrong — that the gang at home would do what was necessary.

An old wrinkly man and an old woman had sat down beside him.

'I was listening to the race,' the old fellow was saying. 'I didn't have a cent to put on him. If I had I would have put it on Trotterine.'

'Our Kevin lost a rake of pounds on him. He said that she had ruined the country . . . Wasn't that a terrible death the two of them got in the car? . . . I heard nothing about that . . . Listen to this! Some guy whose wife has died and he's gone missing, no idea where he is. Here in this city! . . .'

'How come they have no idea?' N. asked.

'They were just looking for information. Any information anybody had to give it to the police. They sent out a call looking for anybody who was in the department store when the robbery took place . . .'

Just at that moment a boy went by calling out the headlines in the evening paper:

'Wallet stolen in department store!'

N. was as distant from the event as he would be from anybody else's life. If he had any apprehension in him at all — and he wasn't without some flutter of fear running through his veins — it was only the kind which he felt while looking at an adventure film. He was involved in such a character with his eyes and with his body, but he could never say that he himself and that other character were the same person; that his tears and his laughter were N.'s tears and laughter. He spoke about what happened as a totally uninvolved person:

'Was it the man whose wife had just died, was it the same person who was robbed in the store?'

'How do you know?' the old man asked.

'Well, I don't, really, but just suppose he was, and suppose that the money for the funeral was in the wallet, and then suppose that he was too ashamed or too afraid, or just fear and shame together, to go home without it . . .'

N.'s voice was dry and tight, like he was reading out a geometrical proposition.

'He'd have nothing to be ashamed of if it was taken clean out of his pocket or swiped from his hand, not his own fault.'

'But just suppose that's all the money he had to buy a habit, a coffin . . .'

'He'd get it on tick.'

'Where?'

'From an undertaker, who else? You don't think he'd get it in a sweet shop, do you?'

'But suppose he didn't know any undertaker?'

'Aaagh! Suppose, suppose, suppose! You're making a song and dance out of it. Suppose he knows nobody. Then, how could he have met his wife? But suppose he didn't know her at all? Suppose it wasn't his wife at all. Suppose his wife hasn't died, either. Suppose there never was any wife at all. Suppose you, me, and this respectable lady . . . You're a right eejit! Somebody will give him some advice, somebody knows something . . .'

'But if it was Saturday evening?'

'What do you want? That she'd be buried Saturday evening! She'll have to be watched and waked until Monday morning . . . Sure thing,' the old man said just as N. was getting up to go. 'What else? It's only culchies want to have someone buried on a Saturday evening! That bogger crowd go mad when they have to stay at home with nothing to listen to, only crows cawing and geese gabbling and then they come here to the city thinking it'll fix them up. I was down in Kilcock once . . . Oh, it's a pity I didn't remember to tell him, as sure as the bird shat in the silk hat that guy knows something, looks as if he does. Hey Mister! Hiya, Mister, you! Come here to me, come here I wantcha? Do you know anything about any credit union? . . . Try some kind, any kind of credit union and you'll see . . .'

N. wasn't involved in any one. He was always too shit scared that some smartass would knobble the savings and he'd lose all his money. Long before his wife was laid up he would spend nights on end trying to prove to her that the shysters in charge of these societies were a bunch of chancers, and her friends also who were doing their best to persuade her to join the Sound-sharp Credit Union on Wishfield Road. He managed to keep her from a boneyard insurance society, as he called it, but her friends got the better of him regarding Soundsharp. Wishfield Road wasn't too far away. He was grateful to the wizened old fella who reminded him. He knew where the union was. He had been around this way before just to prove that the place existed. The door of the building was open, and an old woman whose large head seemed precariously perched on her skinny neck was sitting on a chair cooling it without a care in the world:

'So, your wife's dead so, N. May God have mercy on her soul! She was a great support to the union. We'll have to pass a motion of condolence, have it in the paper by Tuesday evening, maybe . . . She was a member, after all, so she was.'

N. thought by the way she savoured each syllable of that sentence that she was the only member.

'. . . Certainly, we give every help we can to members, but you weren't a member, sure you weren't, N. . . . Saturday is an unfortunate day anyway, really unfortunate, so it is. I have no idea where the committee is today, so I don't. Some of them gone to the races, maybe . . . Why are you looking at me like that, N.? Too true for me. There's no chance you'd get ahold of any of that crowd before the races, so you won't. God only knows where you'd catch up with them. But they'll certainly be back by Monday, so they will. They have to be. There'll be a meeting of the committee on Monday evening. But your wife's savings are subject to the law now, N., and the credit unions are subject to the law also . . .' Of course, the poor woman was scared out of her wits also . . . 'God save us all, a robbery! It's what I was always saying, stay miles away from those big department stores. If only our own credit union could open their own shops with their own money . . . You won't find a bank or a money lender open or available today, so you won't. The small bloodsucking money whores won't leave you a pee-wee's piss and will screw you to the ends of the earth if you don't cough up regularly. You'll have to hang on 'til Monday anyway to get some kind of story . . .'

Wait until Monday, Monday Monday, no good to me, he thought. The buses said so, the piss artists from the boozers said so, the widow Waddel said so, the gutty boys from the side street gangs said so. Did God ordain that we had to wait until Monday? He certainly ordained death, but he never said it had to wait until Monday. N. really wanted to get his hands on his wife's money from the union. He didn't like its building, whose corridors were infested with a musty pall of dust, just like a place where fusty rags were stored. Nor was he happy that the woman had any-thing to do with money. Every penny would have been swiped even by a clueless robber before her big fat turnip head rose up from her skinny heron neck. He didn't mind what she had said about the fancy boys who were skinned at the races. It wouldn't have surprised him one bit if they had put all the union's money on Trotterine . . .

A man in front of him was looking down into the canal. N. didn't have much of a clue what he was looking at, but he noticed that your man was paying particular attention to the area out around him, as if scrutinizing it for detail. N. thought that the time was just about right to ask him a question and to interrupt his own observations.

'What else would you do, like?' he said, without raising his eyes to N. from the muck of the canal. 'Give yourself up to the cops, is that it? They're after you. If they lock you up in the barracks you won't have any choice about going home, and if they let you off, well, that's by their own volition and the will of God, and they can't blame you at home. In that case you'd be helping the police with their enquiries and you couldn't have been at home before that, that is to say, before the time that you actually arrived home, speaking appropriately, of course. Only a nutter, or a complete and utter nutter would hassle you over being delayed, so to speak. But on the other hand, suppose they let you out of the barracks and you didn't go home and they went after you and they found you wandering around and then they brought you back to the barracks again: now, the first question to be asked about this is, just in case that it would keep resurrecting itself again and again, were you in the barracks or out of it, or only there in part, which is to say that you weren't really there? Did you ever think that the full moon would catch up with its own first quarter? 'Cos do you really see what it would be, to put it clumsily, to retreat instead of making progress and even going forward?'

'But doesn't the moon itself actually retreat or back off, I thought anyway?' N. said, his eyes glued to that patch of the river that your man was gawping at.

'You're wrong about that,' the other guy said. 'Even if it appears to be a retreat, a backing off, a surrender on the spot, a return to a place on a journey that he had reached heretofore on his way, that in itself would be deemed to be progress or even going forward. There's no point in putting a tooth in it: any enhancement or magnification or addition to the way things are done is progress or progression in contrast with that which is withering and being reduced and downsizing and being faded away. Because, in all seriousness, there's no point in saying that the whole is greater than the parts. You might, of course, say something like that with regard to width, to breadth, to size, to quantity, but what would you say about that which is not measurable, neither in width nor in breadth nor in size nor in quantity? In your own particular case, the power of the parts is far superior to that of the whole, that part especially where you left the barracks until you returned there is far more important than the whole lot, because it prevents that whole shooting gallery lot from being fulfilled, do you get it, it stops it from being a perfect account, the only way it could pretend to be a full account in and of itself? If you really get it, it's only a flight of fancy, a wishful mooning, a rhapsody of rumour, something imagined without thinking, not anything substantial. In all seriousness we are not comparing the parts with the whole at all, but two separate parts . . .

N. suppressed a painful sigh. Your man wasn't quite as progressive as sighs just yet:

'But it is incumbent on us to return to the beginning and ascertain whether we can discover certain patterns or not. You'll be released from the barracks, that much is clear, let us grant that, that's a given. But you'll be returned to the barracks, and therefore, we're back to what will happen again as sure as the tide comes and goes. We must presume that this will repeat itself *ad finitum*. Or maybe it's just a triangle, an isosceles *delta*, wherein neither its beginning nor its end is known except as a historical *datum.* That is to say, just where you go back to its beginning is precisely where you must start off again to go on to the end. But of course, in this matter, we are entirely bereft of terminology because there is neither beginning nor end, neither progress nor regress. Or to put it another way, we can say that the barracks is that point which you will reach which is nearest to your house after you are released, but that is precisely the same point you were at while you were detained at the same barracks.'

'In the barracks? At my own house?' N. expanded his jaws in a kind of mock yawn and let out a clunk of sound that you couldn't really say was talk, no more than you could call a still-born child a person.

'Did you say, did you say to go home to your house? You will never go home again. You will always be betwixt there and between the barracks. One couldn't conceive or imagine a situation just like it. And just as I have demonstrated you will never know precisely when you are in the barracks and when you are not. That is, of course, as long as barracks and police walk the earth. If barracks and police should vanish from the face of the world, and of course, it is always possible in the fullness of time that they might, this particular case will never cease to be. If you can imagine that you yourself shall not have shucked off these mortal coils, you will be forever and anon fluctuating between two relative points that refer to the aforementioned barracks . . .'

'Are you trying to tell me that I will never be able to go home? Are you trying to say that I don't have a will of my own?'

'Listen to me, you big ignorant slob who hasn't a clue about anything, you left your cop on behind the door and hope that it would all work out when you went home. That's the kind of shit you go on about. I was describing your case according to the unbiased mathematical rules of science, of logic, physics, the latest knowledge of organic life, and then you start bullshitting me about free will and buggering off home . . .'

'Well, yes, if it comes to that, when will I get my wallet back so I can really go home?'

'How do I know when you'll get your wallet? Maybe never. Monday maybe. If you bear with me while I recall some of the other relevant cases —'

'Actually, I don't give a fuck,' N. said, and he left him with his head stuck in a well of rules and regulations that were floating merrily by in the canal.

Actually, N. hadn't the least clue what he should do. That last guy had pissed him off big time. That meeting was so weird that N. began to think that it was a kind of sign. The only thing he could possibly make out from your man was that he was never destined to reach home. No matter what else you might say about him, he wasn't a total thicko. N. was actually delighted to meet somebody just like that told him to go home.

There was another person a little way off sitting by the shallow end of the canal, letting his legs hang down, holding a pipe and looking totally unconcerned. No matter where he was looking, whether into the canal or down on his fly, his eye seemed to be happily somewhere else more or less as if it was dead. If it wasn't for the puffs of smoke which furled from his pipe into the farther air, you might think that he was a kind of statue, even one made out of water. He was the kind of guy who might have some sensible advice, something decent to say, N. thought to himself.

He took the pipe out of his mouth, as if he was going to say something to somebody, hoisted his two legs up on to the path, and went off in the same direction as N., who never supposed he would catch up with him. But after a few minutes it began to dawn on him that the distance between them was getting bigger. Whenever he speeded up or stepped on it, the other guy did the same. N. supposed if he started running the other would run too. Then he remembered a story he had read somewhere. It was about a man whom death promised that if he couldn't catch up with him he would get a longer lease of life. He was being hunted and haunted by death, hunted until he had trapped him in the bottom of a thimble. But it was a tailor's thimble. The man would escape out through the bottom, but death would follow him. The man would dive in again head first, then sneak out once more at the bottom . . . Death had to make some agreement with him at the end of the day, or even when all was said and done.

It appeared to N. there and then that it would be just like that if he took himself out of the barracks, the cops would find him wandering, and then take him back to the barracks and so on and so on forever and ever round and round about. N. had read *Dainty's Dream* in a copy he had borrowed from the library, like other books that would have been very suitable to make a TV programme. *Dainty* had tons of things to torment him in hell, but that was one he didn't have. This was purgatory and beyond, no doubt about it! For ever and always for *saecula saeculorum.*

No matter how much N. thought about it, he couldn't banish from his brain that the guy a while ago wasn't some kind of revelation. He was as someone who could see the horrors of hell down there below him and was alike unto a person who could describe them with poetic diction just as a torturer in purgatory would strip and savage some soul, that is, if this wasn't already hell itself. He strived to remember the details, but could only recall that wild direct look, and the talk which he was convinced was a form of torture. N. quivered with horror. Was this some kind of premonition of all that was to befall him? He looked back over his shoulder, but the man could not be seen anywhere.

The other guy was making a kind of indeterminate shape that wasn't entirely indistinguishable yet from the other shapes all around him, but he was still a good way off. For all that, he reminded N. of somebody. All of a sudden, N. remembered the good guy, the good person who had stood him the drink. Maybe it was him? No sooner had he turned his back on him than N. knew that he had seen his kind of walk before, the gait of his movement, the shrug of his shoulders, even the cut of his face. Maybe he was just trying to avoid N. because he hadn't gone home as he had promised. N. tried to get a grip on himself more than he had done until now. But maybe, who knows, he was the Son of God, fleeing from him, abandoning him, leaving him to the tender mercies of the whip lashers and the torturers . . .

The two passages of the canal stretched before him like Good and Evil. N. preferred to stay on this side, the side he imagined the good man to be. One way or the other he was only trying to pass the time until he could make up his mind what was the best thing to do, especially after all that had passed. Best of all was just to keep walking. The cops would pay less attention to somebody who was on the move. If they caught him moping around, loitering with intent even, they might lock him up and charge him with that last offence. That, or even worse, they might bring him home. That would mean that the gang at home would charge him with a crime that he hadn't even committed. He'd be better off going home himself in his own way and in his own time. The neighbours would have a ball of a time speculating out loud with endless gabble if they saw him coming to his own house accompanied by a cop. That he was fighting, drinking, celebrating his wife's death, crooning away as he stepped over the threshold.

N. stood before a plaque he saw on the wall of a house: St. Vincent de Paul: Francis of Assisi's crowd. That was a good thing. Those two never refused nothing to nobody never. A man of goodly years opened the door, probably a civil servant by the look of his clothes, the way he talked and stood, even by his smell, N. supposed. He avoided N.'s eyes at first, and he did a little impatient tapping with one of his feet on the floor. But in the end, he led him into a room:

'That's a really, really sad story,' he said to N., who thought he got that particular whiff which he associated with civil servants, the kind it is said was the very beginning of decay. 'It's very sad. But it's only one of dozens of such sad stories we get here every day.'

N. didn't really like the idea that his own story was just another common or garden one, a little cellulite drop like thousands of others. N. was ready to reject the case that there were really so many sad stories out there in the world, and he would also refuse to accept that they were all the same or equally deserving of pity, as it was precisely the point that death was common to us all and there was no escape from it. If it was true that all stories were sad stories anyway, it dawned on N. that there was no point in him writing his autobiography . . .

'Why aren't you at home anyway? It's a wonder you haven't gone off home?'

'I was just thinking,' N. said, 'that I'd get some help, a bit of money from you, just for now. Then I'll be on my way home.'

'Vincent de Paul is a society for the poor, for the destitute, for the down-and-out.'

'I'm as down-and-out as the arrow on a prisoner's garb.'

'You should have looked after your money a bit better when you had it. You're not poor.'

'And who do you think is poor so?' N. asked, having to take a grip on the edge of the table to suppress his rising temper.

'We here know full well who is poor and who is not. Aren't you a civil servant? You're being paid by the government, by the people. It's money that's wasted easily—'

'I swear to the Almighty God—'

'Stop that kind of talk . . . The Society of St Vincent de Paul doesn't do things like that . . . What is it we do, you ask? Is that as much as you know? The love of God, charity, and so on. To dress and to feed the body of Christ by dressing and feeding the bodies of his children . . . There's no one here, only myself. The rest of them are all busy, at confession, at devotions. The mission finished tonight in Carn Parish. They want to finish it properly. Anyway, it's usual for the members of the Society to take Saturday night off, the only night they have, really, and to take their wives to play whist . . . The committee won't meet until Saturday night, but I think your case will have to be presented before the Central Committee. Would you like to fill in an application form and I will present it to the committee on Monday?'

'Well, I hope that Monday will go on forever and that you may all go fuck one another whatever happens!' N. said. 'If it ever happens that I have enough money, I'll pay a gang of robbers to fleece ye, and I know that the good guy will forgive me.'

Monday! That's what he would call himself from now on. But he didn't have enough time to chew on that thought. It was more than likely that those righteous pricks from Vincent de Paul would set the cops on him. He jumped on the first bus that came along and got away with the first two stops without paying; but as soon as the conductor came snapping for tickets, N. was gone. The stop was just at a church. This was another sign, N. thought. God was with him: he was directing him precisely to where he could go to confession.

N. began to regret that he let the goodwill that had been

garnered by his meeting with the bollox on the canal to dissipate. The whole world was going to confession in the church. The first thing N. thought of was that a church was the last place that the police would go looking for someone. Weak winking candles were glimmering round about statues, and it was a little gloomy compared to the bright light outside. This soft gentle gloaming seemed to bring him some peace. It was like warm clothes you might put on, having been out in the drenching rain in other gear. He nearly felt like going to confession himself because of the atmosphere of the place and the peace of the people. He felt in a way that going to confession would absolve him of his family commitments, that he would get courage from it, that he would head off home as fearless and as unafraid as if it was one of the gifts of the Holy Spirit . . .

He went back over the events of the day one by one. He wasn't succeeding in persuading himself that it wasn't all entirely his own fault that he was robbed, and of course, everything else flowed from the robbery. There was hardly anybody whom he had told about it that didn't think, either openly or secretly in the back of their minds, that he hadn't asked the robber to rob him. He had to carry the money around with him. The house was the least safe place it could be kept . . .

He saw a kind of dark vault before him. A beam of light coming in at the top. N. imagined that a beam like that would have some symbolic meaning, but his mind was too worn out to go hunting symbols. He thought of *Lead Kindly Light*, a passage of poetry he had learned at school. He was certain that the vault was a side chapel for the coffin. His wife would be brought to a chapel just like that. A few hurried prayers would be said. Everyone would toddle off home then. But he himself N. would not go home. However little the chances that a corpse could possibly exercise any control on the sisters, they'd go completely mad when it wasn't in the house anymore. He'd certainly get more than he bargained for. The brother was a bad one too. He wouldn't be surprised if he had a go to beat the crap out of him. He would, too, if he thought that he'd get away with it. He thought that the best thing for it was to head off down the country with the television crew tonight.

While he was looking into the dark corner he felt what he thought was an enormous *Schlag*, a dull clout, hitting him. He couldn't say it was real, but despite that he felt very uneasy. He slipped out through a side door. He leaned his left hand against the wall of the yard until the effects of the *Schlag* wore off. It was only for a few seconds or thereabouts.

The priest appeared out of nowhere. N. copped that he must be the parish priest because of his age, or the gentle way he approached him, or maybe because of his three-cocked hat, by a kind of easy and positive manner which he exuded as he moved along, as if he had just dismissed the rest of the atmosphere and walked on his own. He was going up and down the yard reading his office. N. told him he'd be fine in a little while. He was already: what he wanted now was enough time to work out how he could soften up the priest. He offered N. a glass of water, which he took. N. hadn't thought he needed water, but it did him good all the same. He told the priest in the yard what he never would tell in confession. He couldn't wait to get to the end of it so he could ask him would he accept the corpse in his church. He wouldn't: the corpse had to be brought to his own parish church. N.'s own parish priest was a gentle kindly reasonable man who would help any parishioner as much as he could. It would give him great pleasure to oblige anyone, especially a man with a corpse . . . But no church could take it tonight. It was too late. He had to wait until Monday . . .

He said a few other things to N. also, some of them unpleasant enough. He refused point blank to give him any money. He had to account for every penny to the parish and to the bishop. The bishop himself was very careful of the finances. As he was leaving, N. didn't remember that so much as that he had mentioned Monday at all. However much he heard it, it hadn't sunk in yet. He started to think that God would have no power on Monday, his power would be in abeyance as the civil service jargon had it, all power would reside in the banks, graveyards, undertakers, and other weird places. There would be no point in praying to God on Monday. You'd have to pray to those other weird people and places . . .

N.'s feeling that he needed to go to confession had completely vanished. He had confessed to so many people since the early morning. What they all wanted to say to him was that it was his own fault. How could they possibly know it was his fault any more than it was the policeman's not to be in the garden when the traitor squealed. Only one person forgave N., the guy who bought him the drink he was gasping for along with dispensing his forgiveness. He bought him whiskey: the priest gave him piss water. What the others really were gagging to say was that he was too miserable and too guilty to look for forgiveness from God, or that God would even listen to him. The man who forgave him never hinted or implied that he belonged to any church or had any official love of God. Christ was always denying the formal churches, the spiritually barren. Christ would never have been an officer in a credit union, in St. Vincent de Paul . . . or a priest . . .

A bit of a crowd had gathered around the bridge. Some of them were on their way out of the pub, others on their way in. One way or the other they all delayed a little to listen to a hymn being sung by members of the Salvation Army on the other side of the street. N. headed over to them. He remembered that he was to call them about his wife's clothes earlier in the day. The main Army man listened carefully to his story and was very sympathetic. He offered him a place for the night and a bite to eat and a sup to drink. He wasn't so sure about giving him any money. He couldn't really decide himself. Somebody higher up the food chain would settle it, but it would have to be postponed until Monday, anyway.

'Until Monday!' N. exclaimed, the patience that he had learned with some effort in the civil service was only a fragile flap against the flood. 'But why Monday?'

'Because this is Saturday night and tomorrow is Sunday, the Sabbath.'

'But did Christ ever observe the Sabbath? He cured people on the Sabbath. He did works of mercy on the Sabbath. He stuffed the craw thumpers and the holy Marys with the seven devils when they were going on endlessly sickula sickulorum about the Sabbath. But why do you have to wait for your boss? If you are a Christian as good as anyone why don't you just sink your hand in your own pocket . . .'

'And 'twould come out just as empty. I can't help it, my good fellow. I'm only telling you how it is. I can't do anything about it. It's just the way things are.'

People were beginning to gather around, noticing what was going on. The Salvation Army man wasn't entirely comfortable, and he slithered off the first chance he had without making it look like he was abandoning the scene. Somebody grabbed N.'s sleeve. Because there were so many people thronging around and hassling him, he really noticed only his two eyes.

'Isn't it a pity altogether,' he said to N. 'And to think that I just did exactly the same for another man already today. If I only knew two hours ago . . . She'd have gone to the church tonight . . . Oh, I don't really know. It's too late now anyway . . .'

He looked at his watch as if he was having doubts about what he had just said.

'That's just it. If only I had known about it even just two hours ago! Isn't it a real pity you didn't come to see me? . . . You didn't know about me? Ah, isn't that terrible altogether! She'd be laid out no bother in the church by now and you'd be settled back at home. If you're ever in any trouble like this again, be sure to let me know. Here's my number . . .'

As N. was looking at his watch the man vanished. N. took off briskly in the direction where he thought the man had gone, and wandered in and out of the streets round about, but there wasn't a sign of your man. He looked in the pub. Asked about him. It was then that he realized that he had ever only noticed his eyes. They were a special kind of eyes. They were gentle and sympathetic, but like precious stones the look in them switched back and forth as if they were hiding some secret. One way or the other those eyes were lost as the man had his back turned to him. It seemed to N. that he had taken off just as quickly as the guy at the canal just a while before. It was another piece of good fortune that had been mysteriously swiped from him. There were so many things that N. would have loved to ask him.

He'd certainly tell him how to clear up the mess he was in right now. N. could only remember the cut of his eyes. Despite that he was more clearly etched in his mind than the good guy or that other person he met along the canal. He was the first person today who knew how to get N. out of his predicament. He was a person, indeed a being, like unto 'the helper,' the 'Do-Gooder' from the heroic stories who would tell you how to escape from all those scrapes and dangers you were ever in. He was the reincarnation without any reservations of the good man. It was unlikely he would meet anyone like him again. N. was afraid that too many people had heard his story in the last hour, and especially when he was talking to 'the Do-Gooder,' as he now dubbed him. During the day he had never told anybody, only when necessary, and then to somebody that he thought he could trust. But something he couldn't quite grasp was bugging him, something he couldn't quite get despite all the ears which had heard his story, apart from the ears of this one man.

While N. was fidgeting with the bit of paper, he decided he would call his number. He would hardly have got home yet. He headed back towards the church. He would be safer there. It would be a disaster if they caught up with him now when he was nearly home. N. knew he was always a bit superstitious. Everything landed on him together in one go, both the good and the bad.

He felt a bit strange about the confession he was going to make a while back, for all the good he was going to get from it. More superstition, he supposed. There was no better way to dissolve your problems than to let them slip through the invisible fingers of God. And despite this, it was so easy to solve things in the simplest possible way here and now at the level of the human. The man who had given him the telephone number was working at this level, the very 'Do-Gooder' himself. A whole plethora of clichés swarmed into N.'s mind. His wife used to say that those clichés were the basis for all of his actions. Yet more offspring of his family of clichés, N. thought. It wasn't what you knew, it was who you knew. You could do anything if you knew the right person who knew the right people! There you have it: the man who gave him the number didn't say a squeak about Monday!

N. spent the best part of many quarter-hours thinking about the magical properties that the right person would have, the way he could bring heaven down to earth and raise earth up to the same level as heaven so that heaven would be earth and earth heaven! In the midst of this most appropriate reverie one of these entirely inappropriate clichés sneaked its way into his mind from somewhere, 'There is a divinity that shapes our ends.' Maybe someone from the office mouthed that one. Maybe the same one who always wondered why God in his glory had expended so much trouble in inventing the arse, or why he gave so much importance to a part that you'd never imagine God had created, a shapeless useless blemish apart from the fact that it had a waste pipe for an engine. Then he'd shake his head regretfully: 'Just like any bureaucracy it would seem the bureaucracy above was a little unsure of itself also! . . .'

N. found a telephone. It spent a long time ringing but there was no answer. He spent half an hour dossing around the place and then rang again. The same thing. N. couldn't really make up his mind whether he was disappointed or not. He thought that if somebody could dial up God in heaven, it would go on ringing and ringing without answer forever and ever amen, also. It was a kind of a sign that there was nothing he could do now. The last rope had finally been cut . . .

N. remembered he should ring the television crew again to remind them that he would be doing the commentary that evening. Maybe Colm might have heard the SOS. In that case N.

would just say to him that no matter how much he wanted to stay at home, he wouldn't because he had signed a contract to do the work. He'd meet them on their way out of the city at the Jolly Roger just beside the bridge. That's where they had arranged to meet. Colm told him it would be just as easy to collect him at his home, so he needn't bother his barney to come as far as the Jolly Roger. N. had another meeting at the pub, so he had to go there anyway.

N. understood immediately that Colm hadn't got the SOS. That was all the better. N. was fairly certain that none of the others had got it either. He spent five minutes reminding himself of another cliché: no television person ever heard or watched any television programme except his own programme, or even anything except his own bit of his own programme. N. thought he wouldn't mind going to a barber to get cut, cleaned, shaved, and shaped up, but he realized he didn't have enough cash. But if it was necessary, Colm would commandeer him into a barber before they left the city, and it would all be put on the bill . . .

N. took the shortcut through the backstreets to the Jolly Roger. More than ever he didn't want to be caught now before he did the commentary. The Jolly Roger was safe enough, but not far enough away . . .

As he was settling himself into the big plush fancy car, Colm's secretary, blond Squimzy, whispered in his ear that her boss was like a bear with a sore head that the north wind had knocked off. He himself had been blown from one confused crisis to another since morning: no money, fear, contradictory advice, despair, ennui: every bee buzzing in his business trying to prick and to sting him until he imagined himself locked in a coffin that was closing in upon him and that there was no way out. N. would tell his friends in the office and his neighbours about the luxury and the size of the car just to make them jealous, if nothing else was happening. It was a kind of achievement in itself just to sit in a car in luscious luxury like this with all its flash and fancy, something that none of them would ever experience. The minister couldn't get anyone much better, even the minister in his own department. N. began to see it as an extension of his own personality, like a doppelgänger or a spooky wraith, or indeed as a badge of heroism or an Olympic medal around his neck. He thought once of saying something like that in the office and he regretted that the smartass civil servant had shut him up with one of his quips: 'You'd need two arses to get full value from that kind of luxury.'

N. could be occasionally gripped by an irrational fear in this car, or even one like it. He would imagine that the car was about to begin to shrink, to shrivel like a tax-screwed employee, or that it would vanish into itself like a snail's shell, like the brittle carapace of a crawly, or the brittle crust of a coffin in which there was really no hell to which any torture could be assigned—neither the Hell of *Dainty* or any other—only a hell which closed crushingly in on him bit by bit without end. But other times his fear was far more troubling than that, just the fear that his kind of life would end, maybe quite suddenly without warning, and that ever-surrounding darkness would be his real and only presence henceforth. It would be like losing an arm, or a foot, or a leg, or an eye . . .

This fear haunted him tonight. It was too true: Colm was in a bad bitch of a mood. He was cursing and fucking and bejaysus-ing like wood chips flying off a saw. Nobody else had a chance to open their mouths . . .

'This fucking bogplace shithole here,' he said, 'we have to get our asses down here this time of day because of some shitehawk pissartist suckslob TD who wants us the only time it fucking suits him and his fucking cunning cuntconvent of a cuntstituency.'

'Yea, right so, certainly,' N. said sleepily, as the welcoming laziness of his relaxed body sought to cross the threshold be-tween being half awake and totally zonked out asleep. 'The right person would be able to do it,' he said, without calling upon any part of his body to awaken, except his tongue and his mouth.

'What kind of total incoherent asshole bullshit is that you're spouting? I could easily chuck you out on your head until you actually realized whether you were better off drowning in a vat of vomit or sclambering up on a slush hill of shite.'

N. woke up, every single part of him. He was kept alive that time by the small shock of electricity which shot through him when Squimzy grabbed his hand in hers.

The TD Bootleg was there in his new suit waiting for them, holding forth saying exactly the same as had to be said every time anything had to be said anywhere or anytime.

'It'll give these poor hoors a great lift if they are seen on TV,' he said.

'And to others also,' Colm said without as much of a thought, flicking the butt of his fag away as easily as the flighty bird deposited his little load on a fancy hat.

'Let's get them all in the picture for a start,' Bootleg said.

'Excuse me now, Deputy Bootleg,' Colm said, 'this is not exactly a local picture of the constituency workers. I'm in charge here. We are going to show the extent of the bog, its size, its length, how far away it reaches. And of course, how deep it goes also, but I'm afraid our cameras will not be able to reveal the horrors of those depths. If we ever get a camera like that it's most likely to plumb the depths of Leinster House and we'll be next. We can only go on about what's happening round about here right now. The guts of it will have to wait, but we might have to scrape the surface while we're here'; he was staring with venom at Bootleg: 'but let N. talk first.'

'I actually thought,' Bootleg said, 'that it would be better if . . .'

'I'm the one to decide what is best and what is not, Deputy Bootleg.'

N. didn't actually like the way Colm went straight for the throat. He was half afraid that Bootleg had the authority to fire him, or at least to transfer or to demote him along the way. He could be a bit of a bollox with everyone, just as Colm knew. But he had a good heart. They often thought if he ever changed his ways that his replacement would need a totally new broom and that no part-timer would ever again get a look-in . . .

'Camera ready here . . . over here . . . and here . . . Say a few words, N., just to check voice level. Something about the importance of bogs to Ireland and how it was ever thus and that things will be much better from now on than they ever were . . . Ready so! . . . Off you go until we check . . .'

'People always cut turf in Ireland until today.' There was nothing unusual about that, but N. dwelled a while on the word 'today,' something which made it quite magical and prophetic, as if it was some other person who was loosening his tongue and moving his mouth: 'but no sod will be turned nor any grave dug until Monday.'

'Until Monday, did you say, or until some day? But why would you say either of them? . . . Until Monday you said, so . . . Yes, that's true, no grave will be dug . . . Not until the ends of the earth! But nevertheless, and all the same . . .'

N. carried on his commentary under Colm's direction without even a glitch. He was rabbiting on about the great machines which would have been on the screen other times, except that they weren't there just then, as it happened:

'But they will be again on Monday,' N. declaimed, as if he were a prophet.

'Fuck you and all that shite that you're on about! Whatever came into your head to mention Monday one way or the other. What's this about Monday that's pissing you off? But you know, you're probably right. We could have just as well come here on Monday as any other day if we were coming at all. But the way it was, Bootleg's arselickers and spongers and hangersonners couldn't keep him even one hour away from the daily diarrhea, especially as it wasn't his own bog people who were doing the programme. But I'm not sure, N., if you could be here yourself either, on Monday morning.'

Colm hardly said a word on the way back.

'We won't do a tap again until Monday,' he said once, only with an ugly grin that would have pained the person who had heard or had seen it. 'I made a total fuck up, a pig's arse, a continental cock up of the film. I wouldn't give Bootleg the steam of my piss, the heap of shit. He can kiss my arse, his fat full ancient awfully Offaly arse, and who knows, maybe an arse hero might be arse growing out of the arse bog by now . . .'

This kind of dirty talk upset N. Somebody who knew Colm's real feelings would spill it to Bootleg, or it would travel from one gossip to another gossip until it reached his ears in the end. N. thought just for the sake of peace and goodwill and to keep everyone on side they should let Bootleg alone also. When he intimated as much to Colm as they were about to leave the boggers, he gave him a savage look:

'I wouldn't leave him the steam of the stool off my shite, even if he was gagging for it, despite all the lumps of frozen piss shite cack lumps he has already. But, of course, he doesn't have to look for that anyway, all he has to do is to look into his own piss cum personality . . .

Colm let Squimzy off at her own place and was about to bomb off again when he thought he heard N. chatting her up at the door.

'Are you in or are you out,' he shouted as nastily as N. had ever heard him. 'Out so! Well then, fuck off out! . . .' He slammed the door and N. felt in his innards that he too was being slammed out 'into eternal darkness,' as he said to himself.

N. felt like bursting out crying. Why was it he had done nothing during the day? He was neither here nor there, like a thirsty man glugging for a drop of water but when he found it he noticed he had left his hands behind in some place that he had completely forgotten.

'My wife has died,' he blurted out to Squimzy in one gulp of breath. That's when he realized he had to tell her.

'Poor N.,' she said as she opened the door, leaving it slightly ajar. Then she said back to N.:

'Don't make any noise on the stairs . . . Tell me, is your heart broken, N.?' she said, fumbling around for the light switch next to the door, but then, without waiting for an answer: 'I suppose you haven't eaten anything since this morning, or drunk anything — not much anyway. That was obvious tonight. I really felt for you. You don't believe me. Your eyes had vanished into their sockets, and the way you spoke, you were like somebody just mouthing someone else's words. Colm was a total prick and the arsehole of a prick all together. Did he call Bootleg a boghole bollox or something like that? He'll have to scrub that from the record. Can't blame him entirely, though. His heart is in the right place and he goes totally ballistic when know-nothing nobodies stick their nose into his business. Hang on a minute now, and I'll have something for you.'

A mountain of sandwiches grew around his knife and fork.

'Here,' she said, taking out a bottle of gin which was full to the gills out of a cupboard, 'pour out a drop for me also. Better drink first and eat afterwards. I have only one small miserable bottle of tonic, but we can slip that into the tea.'

'You were never short of whatever was needed,' N. said, as he felt he had to say something, and this phrase just jumped out of his mouth. In a little while a few other phrases and clichés came easily, helped by the food and the drink.

'I feel a bit loosened up again, thanks to you.'

'Even though she has passed away,' Squimzy said.

N. was a bit too full, too woozy with booze to begin to wrestle with something like this. But it was enough to get him going back over the unfortunate events of the day, even if he was still smart enough not to say anything to let her think he was trying to cadge money from her. He knew full well what he might want, but what he would never get. Colm always said that Squimzy was a sort of predated cheque, milking every trick she could pull off (and pull off she could) with public relations officers, as well as playing her games with hopeful TV types, and hoping that those hopeless hapless lot of ginks might happen to buy her a drink, but she had to admit that they were getting scarcer and more scarcer all the time. N. would have to take a fat slice from his own fees to defend her against the bloodsucking landlord who gave her a week's notice to quit her room regularly.

N. reflected on his own life. Readers would like to know about it. But could he ever publish it? If he did, he was sure that the sisters would have him in court to disgrace themselves and himself too, as well as trying to get their grubby paws on all the costs. He then noticed that her eyes had gone a bit dead, not like they usually were. There was only a drop left in the tonic, they didn't bother making tea, and the gin staring at Squimzy was beginning to get to her. In the end, she grabbed him by the wrist, telling him to keep the glass up to his lips, while her eyes were completely closed by now. Then she got up suddenly, whipped off the kind of loose apron she wore in the house, a covering which N. called a 'shield,' as he couldn't think of any other exact name for it. 'I don't know why I call it a "shield,"' he'd say, 'I suppose a shield to keep your clothes from getting dirty, and then, it also looks forbidding enough to act as a chastity belt, if that's not exactly what it is.'

She turned down the bedclothes, yanked down her blue slacks around her knees, which she stuck up in the air, and lay back. N. sat on the side of the bed and poured out another measure, which made her cough and splutter when he brought it to her lips. But then her breathing came back to normal again. Her hand stretched out groping to find a comb, or so she said, but just happened to grab his.

N.'s half-woozy mind imagined Venice with its watery canals, where the good guy wandered around in many disguises. He felt like Columbus trying to find a sailor to go ashore on a new island. Then he became like the Ancient Mariner, whom N. could think of only as a miserable wretch screaming from below in the sea: 'What else would you do but give yourself up to the police? . . .' Then he escaped from that horror only to become a wandering sailor all on his own in a small boat out on the ocean. N. thought he would have to put that in his story. Then he came to a desert island. As soon as he planted a foot on the shore his shape changed—he turned into a green man! But he underwent yet another change. He was himself, N. all the time. He himself N., the mean, concupiscent, greedy, lazy, angry, lascivious N., he was the good guy! And he had the island all to himself. And there was no evil sinful human vessel round about to lead him into temptation, to destroy his innocence. Nothing to think about except his own good decent humanity, and to enjoy thinking about it forever! Neither money nor drink nor anger nor dirty intentions to interfere with his own good thoughts. It could only be that he would get fed up of them! And he'd be better off as a bad guy, banished from this holy island, back sailing on the sea of sin, back to the corrupt and wicked island of wisdom . . .

He was looking through a golden mist at the ship in which he had been travelling:

A ship from Valparaiso came

And in the Bay her sails were furled . . .

N. had no idea how his mind had become so obsessed with water. Some kind of retribution from *Dainty* for abandoning the holy isle. Water, water everywhere, a big expanse of water, and he sailing over and back across it. There was something stuck in his body: something like extra limbs: ropes, beams, and sails from the boat, what else?

Over the golden pools of sleep

She went long since with golden spars,

Into the night empurpled deep
And traced her legend on the stars.

He would trace them. In the story of his life. On the radio, the television. And why wouldn't he? Wouldn't it be far more enjoyable than the stinking bog, the arsehole of Ireland. He was just about to read it when he was grabbed by the scruff of his neck—The Bootleg, the Buttleg, the filthy frog bogger, and got a kick up the arse that nearly went through him sending him down out of the radio! Fuck! Fuck you Buttlegger, Buttamore! A cracked condom on your prick, Bootleg! Fuck! . . .

N. came to. He only had the slightest gossamer memory of a dream, but he well knew that Valparaiso figured in it and he was bursting his gut trying to get a radio version together when he woke up. When he was fully aware it dawned on him that his Valparaiso wasn't at all bad. He'd have to think of other tricks and stratagems if the Bootleg butter lick was going to censor his TV program. He was trying to imagine how he would describe 'the darkling city, bright as a jewel'—a city of purse snatchers and pickpockets—when the shades of sleep came again upon him.

And it was a disturbed sleep. He was looking down into the canal, searching for something, and then once more unable to lift up his eyes. He was stuck in a black hole or in a gouged gulch. He couldn't make out why he was trapped there. Taking a piss, maybe, or shaking hands with the idle unemployed. But it was much more likely they were keeping him against his will.

Above him, a man, not unlike the Bootleg himself was threatening and warning above him that he should never sell his soul.

Be that as it may, and however he happened to be there, he was here now, and had no idea how to get out. As soon as he would lift one leg, the other would be stuck fast. And then, just after, he failed to get any leg out of any hole. He offered whatever it was worth to some guy to pluck him out of the bog hole. He produced his wallet just as a guarantee. But the guy swipes his wallet and makes off with whatever he has in it! N. could feel himself slipping and sliding even deeper into the hole. There was a real sourpuss woman laid in the coffin, hair greyed and big fat butt. N. was about to lie down beside a flash of flesh which was incomparable in terms of flab. Just like that, the flab of flesh became in a dark flash like unto the man from the Vincent de Paul, but not quite. Through the fog of the bog and the mug of the muck, N. recognized the priest. He bellowed to N. that he should make his confession and peace with God, because he didn't have much time. Sure enough, here he was approaching as a policeman with rattling handcuffs . . .

N. woke up with a start. Squimzy was awake too: 'Do you know what? You recited every single poem that was ever in my books at school . . . And Colm would give anything for your fucking, farting, and fullshitting . . . that I don't know. Please don't ask me that, N. . . . . Every bit, as well as the Buttass Bootleg. And the Vincent de Paul, the Salvation Army, priests, horses, arses . . .'

He'd need a long passionate session on Squimzy's lustrous lascivious lips to crack that one and to bring him back to earth.

The old pagan thing within him got him back to some kind of sense. In the corners of the room the brightness was clonking the darkness. N. didn't budge until some of the sunlight had bathed the room. Then he put the bedclothes across Squimzy's long legs, which had played their game with gusto in their time, but which were now hardly distinguishable from the bedsheets in the ghostly white of the pale morning dew.

They got him thinking about other things, mostly unpleasant: the heater in the department store, the watery wan of mushy mushrooms, tired candles that had been saved for years to place next to a corpse, planks or boards that still retained fine sawdust after fresh shaving. It was pretty obvious that Squimzy wasn't eating the healthiest food. What was she doing with her salary? She wasn't coughing up to some landlord, or even splashing out on the shops. She certainly wasn't spending it on clothes, as she was half naked most of the time. Nor on drink. She drank alright, but she didn't spend much of her own money.

N. couldn't banish his memory of the programmes. He had a vague recollection of a coffin somewhere in his dreams. This put the shits on him a bit, and he settled the clothes back on Squimzy without waking her. He swilled back the remains of the gin, which sent a shot through his body, like barbed wire being scraped across his gut. He made some strong tea and drank it down in one gulp, jolting him only long enough to get his breath back. He wanted to cast his eyes back towards the bed, a big wide comfortable bed, which despite everything had provided him with a good night's sleep, at least. He didn't really know why he didn't want to look at Squimzy. She was the colour of a plank of wood, a bleached pale presence beneath her carefully reddened makeup, something he hadn't quite noticed until now. It was the gin, he said to himself, the gin set his head dancing on his shoulders. He crawled quietly down the stairs and carefully drew the door closed behind him . . .

The raw flowing air of the morning kicked the sludge of the booze out of his head.

When he found himself out on the suburban street with nobody much around, it dawned on him that he didn't have to leave Squimzy's place at all until much later, when the morning had woken up and there would be many more than him out and about. He wasn't too worried about bumping into a cop while wandering around. He'd probably understand that he was a late-night reveler making his weary way home after a piss-up. The cop would probably even be jealous: the whole world and betty martin were at it in their warm beds except him. The cop himself would be fairly knackered by now not to bother his butt too much with anyone, unless he caught somebody red-handed so to speak in flagrant delinquency trying to smash a window, for example, or pissing or having a crap against a convent wall. In that last case he would most likely have let him off, having thumped some of the shite out of him.

The pigs in the car were the problem. They didn't even have to stir their arses to do anything in order to question someone and haul him into the barracks. After all, they had to show that they were working. If there had been some murder, or a robbery or a brawl or a rape in their district which they should have seen but didn't. End of shift was always their eleventh hour; they would have expected to have made some arrests at least by then.

N. slinked away through the narrow lanes where cars could not follow, trying to get away as far as he was able. He seemed to see some kind of end in sight, even if it was entirely vague, and if his legs kept going. He didn't delay too much, nor did he speed along, but avoided every chance that maybe someone would try to slow him up. It would be even worse to catch up with him today than it had been yesterday. Yesterday's sins were those of that day's only; today's went all the way to the end of the night. Nor did he feel entirely not guilty like he did yesterday.

He was imagining the end of his journey through a dense labyrinth of lanes and alleys and back passageways. The Do-Gooder, whoever he was, that is who he needed. He was there all the time, only to find him out. If he got him in time, he would certainly be his saviour. Whoever said that today was not his lucky day? Who said he couldn't do something great today that he couldn't do yesterday? There was nothing you couldn't do when God was on your side.

N. said an act of contrition to God for his years of being a complete bollox. But he also knew that he could have been a much bigger prick. Like, suppose that he had swiped somebody's wallet and that was all they had in the whole wide world? God had promised especial punishment for those who were cruel to widows . . . Squimzy had said to him that God understood better than anyone else. There were many sins that God really didn't give a toss about, no more than one took any notice of an ad on television; but then, you'd never know, as soon as something popped up on his own God Channel and grabbed his attention he was all ears, nose out front, eyes popping, lips salivating, ready for anything . . . By all accounts, God and Squimzy had a good understanding. But you couldn't really trust her. N. had some-thing against her because she drank gin. That was all very well last night, of course. She gave him food, drink, shelter, and the rest of it. If it hadn't been for her, he would be arrested and dumped in a cell by now.

For some reason he wasn't getting anywhere along the by-ways and lanes any more. These roads were all for cars. N. asked himself why for fuck's sake he was putting himself in the way of the cops at this stage. The Do-Gooder helpmate. He kind of had it locked away in the recesses of his mind to search him out, to be in a place where he could call on him. He wasn't entirely certain that he wasn't heading towards the bridge where he had been the other evening, the bridge where he had met the Do-Gooder before. But the Do-Gooder could be here, or there, or anywhere just as easily.

He was up and down and round about
He was climbing up the spout.
Went round the world on a razzamatazz
But came back to where he was.

You could get him anywhere, or call him from wherever.

N. intended to call him later, but not to leave it so late that he would be gone out. He dug deep in his pockets but couldn't find his number. It should have pissed him off more when he thought that maybe it fell out of his pocket in Squimzy's place. Squimzy was, of course, his occasion of sin, his fatal weakness, what with her gin and her messing and all the rest of it. And then again, in a flash, it dawned on him that Squimzy's place, nor nowhere else, had nothing to do with it. Things were as they were. That number should not be available just to any old knacker, just like you might get hold of the number of a grocer, or a doctor, or an undertaker, after all he was special. N.'s courage hadn't weakened one bit. That great good God who had already sent him the Do-Gooder, and after that Squimzy, he could put many more in his way. No need to go looking for them. Actually, it would be a pure waste of time to go looking for them. He would have to hold fast and just bear with it until God sent him someone who would tell him what to do, and then he could go off home and fix all the stuff that needed fixing. If the worst came to the worst, he could always use the excuse he had concocted for yesterday again today.

He came out onto a road he didn't recognize, one that was bigger than any other he had seen yet this morning. There was a spacious park with a big fancy-looking house in a bit across from him at the end of the road. There were trees, bushes, and hedgerows dotted throughout the park. N. thought that this was a great chance for someone like him to hide under a bush or a shrub and wait until the city woke up on this particular Sunday morning. It looked like the best option he had.

He moseyed around the edge until he got to a part of the

perimeter that was low enough to hop over. He didn't look too closely at the bush. It was enough that it was sufficiently leafy to give shelter and he could hardly be seen from the road, or from the house, if it came to that. He never felt like an outlaw on the run until now! What the hell would they say in the office? Some of them would certainly want him fired. Anyway, this is exactly what he had to do. As he hunkered in under the bush, the dew of the morning early and the bite in the air and the clammy ground on which he lay under the dense growth of the foliage which blocked out the heat all sent a shiver of cold through his body. He stuck his head out on one side. The bright eye of the sun would wink at him there when it rose in the east.

The cold and the worry didn't last too long. He soon felt enveloped by a warm embrace of safety which massaged his weary and stiffened limbs as with an oil of kindness. He didn't get much peace last night what with Squimzy on the one hand and the ghouls who roamed through his dreams on the other. He tried to bring back that dream which he had always intended to reconstruct. He just had to remember it until he got a chance to scribble it down. Part of his sleep he spent on that ship to Valparaiso, or coming back from there. More's the pity it wasn't true. That would solve just about everything. But that ship had its own problems. It entered a dead sea of calm. It was like unto a painted ocean in its deadness, hot under a copper sky so that everybody fell into a dull deep sleep from which they could not easily awaken. But it wasn't a peaceful sleep. N. could sense the long spooky hand stretching down the chimney, clawing around for his wallet. N. could feel the way he was completely shivering scared even in his sleep. But it was only Squimzy wrapping her body around herself all the more tightly. Then he could see a bed with a corpse folded and bent before him. He could barely see the corpse's eyes. But he could see the face which had become the blank colour of wet sand. Before his eyes the sand began to take on a definite colour — it was turning black. There were a few women standing around. One of them was pointing her finger at the eyes in the bed. Now they were quite clear to him, more alive than they ever were, he thought. They were small little eyes even when she was alive.

'They'll never ever close now,' the reproachful finger one said, 'because they weren't closed at the right time. Nor will they be able to straighten her out. She's completely knotted. How'll they manage to stuff her into the coffin? . . . They'll have to make a special one now. But you could never make a coffin that would fit her in the way she's all in a heap of lumps.'

'Bit by bitch, inch by pinch,' the other one said, and let out a mad roar of laughter while looking at N. 'Rattle her bones into little pieces and then they'll fit in any box.'

N. imagined a big metal mallet swimming towards him, but he backed off in order to duck it.

'We have all heard about,' the first one said, 'we have all heard about the prodigal son who got money from his father and fecked off to make his fortune, or even to find himself. No matter how bad he was he didn't choose to chase loose women or harry whores the night his wife died.'

N. snapped out of his sleep and thought that Squimzy was lying there beside him, at least for a while — as the sun which was peeping through the roots of the bush was blinding him. Apart from the sun, another zealous eye was staring at him. It wasn't difficult to deduce from the long stick waving about in the man's hand that he was some kind of security bod.

'Hey, you won't give me up to the cops, will you?' N. said, rather uselessly trying to shake off the man's firm grip on his shoulder.

'What are you trying to do?'

'Get away from the cops.'

'What crime have you committed?'

'What crime have I committed?'

'What do you think? What have you done? 'Tis perfectly obvious, written on your face. And your flap down below opened out as far up as your mouth.'

It was true. N. had forgotten to zip himself up as he left Squimzy's place. 'It could happen to a parish priest, my good man . . .'

The security bod, the night watchman, made a grunting noise which might have been agreeing with him or not, but he said nothing.

'It's all true, my good sir, I have done nothing wrong. Wrong things were done to me. Like being robbed yesterday.'

'Why then are you on the run from the police?'

'Yes, that's true. There's an SOS out . . .'

'I heard something yesterday, something about a man whose wife had died.'

'And the cops are after me to take me back.'

Then he tried to tell his story to the watchman, even though both worry and his rickety limbs brought home to him that he hadn't the least clue what he was up to, or looking for.

'One way or the other,' the watchman said, 'you can't hang about here. That building over there is a hostel for young women, young women who are working all over the city. I'm sure it would be a wonder to behold if one of them peeped out of her window in the early morning light to see your big open flap staring out at her as the sun came up . . . And, hey, don't think that you are the first person I nabbed around here. But I don't catch most of them when they are asleep. There's another hostel for clerical students behind that, over there. There's a small gate out the back in front of the hostel. I lock that gate every night, it's the first thing I do, but there's still one smartass who manages to open it, no matter what. These temptresses have their own tricks, making signals across to the guys, flashing the lights at the back of their place on and off. I often caught one of them blackguards trying to climb in through the window. Bad enough as it is, and as good-looking as some of them are, many of them, those women are heretics, real black Protestant heretics. Only last week I grabbed one of the clerical students up to his balls going through the window. I hauled him out. He said nothing but took a grip on my throat. I was some tough boyo myself once upon a time, even if I say so myself. I was a champion in the army. I was that, and as hard as nails. I could recite every word of *The Midnight Court*, top of my tongue . . .'

'O my God, did you really know that?' N. asked, although he hadn't the least clue what it was, except it must have been something really bad.

'God's honest truth,' the watchman said. 'Them women there were often nearly mauling me begging me to recite it, to write it out for them, but then since I got this job . . .'

'You dealt with the student, anyway,' N. said, 'it was coming to him, and he deserved it.'

'You wouldn't believe it, my good man, nor anyone else either, nor me neither if I hadn't done it. What do you think he did, he cocked his bum at me? I swear to Jesus. In the window he plops, pulls it down, and locks it from the inside. I was betwixt and between two minds all night whether I would squeal on him or not. The way I looked at it, it would be one big hullaballoo and unholy hassle if I shopped him in. "Aha, let him be," I said to myself, "It's all much of a muchness. Maybe I'll toddle over to his president in the morning and lay it out . . ." But then again, I thought it was strange the way he was able to escape my clutches. I was maybe getting a little bit scared of him. Maybe he had some special divine gift to be able to pull that off. In the morning I went back over to the window he had gone back through, and gave it a knock:

'"You should have enough of that warm bed and board by

now," I said. Out he comes. I grabbed him and gave him one big thump. He was as quiet as a lamb. Crawled away home as cowed as a drowned puppy. "No doubt about it, you have enough of the old up-and-at-it rough-and-tumble for a good while yet," I says. God save us all, just think somebody like him allowed to be a priest of Holy God's! It beats me. Then it dawned on me that he'd be going on the missions to some foreign field and he'd be good enough for some of them blacks, anyway. There were many saints who spent their lives repenting because of the wild oats they had sown in their youth. And who knows, maybe he left something worthwhile after him — he was certainly long enough at it — maybe even another little priest . . . But I'll tell you this much. I don't know if it is something new that's happening now or not. May God forgive me for even thinking it! I think priests should be allowed to marry. Watchmen like me will never get a night's peace until they do. Either that or they pass a law to castrate them all . . . every single one of them gelded up to their goolies. May God forgive me! I don't think you could even trust the pope, for all his talk . . .'

All this talk seemed to have softened the watchman's opinion of N. It had brought familiarity and flexibility to the cold steel of duty. He brought N. back into his lodge and prepared something decent to eat. N. realized that he was another 'good one,' and that God was preparing the way before him. N. had given him a precise enough account of what had happened to him, apart from that bit about Squimzy. He thought that it wouldn't be quite appropriate to spill that stuff to a Co-Adjutant of God's, like this guy. Getting advice from him was like getting it from the Do-Gooder himself.

'You know my own business now just as well as I do myself,' N. said to him. 'I can't wait to get home now. What do you think I should do so that I can go home in the best possible way?'

'I don't know,' the watchman said, 'actually I don't really know. May God guide you anyway. As you said yourself, as it has gone this far, it might be just as well to postpone the return until tomorrow. They'll manage alright at home. They just have to. What I'd suggest is to go to Mass and ask God for guidance. If he thinks going home is the best thing to do now, he'll send you an angel to light your way. You'll never believe it, but I've often been here in this lodge in the middle of the night, and there the angel would be at the door and all I'd have to do is to follow him as far as the window—and there were so many windows, you better believe it!—over in the big building just in time to grab a clerical student by the heels and haul him legs first out of some young one's room, some one of those heretics. And do you see now that I realised that it was no angel that was guiding me that night when I caught the little knacker, it just came to me unbidden, all off my own bat. And that it was a sign that maybe it was God's will that I shouldn't squeal on him. No doubt about it, my job here is a very special one. If God doesn't look after his own, who will do it for him? But listen to me, N., if you hope that the police won't notice you, you should go and wash and shave yourself. There's a place here . . .'

As he was heading down towards the church, N. wasn't in any way scared of the law. He was meeting good decent people. Whatever he did, it was God's will. It seemed as if there were helpful and obliging angels all around wherever somebody could see them. He recalled that he had met an angel incarnate the evening before. N. had often heard that there were things that angels could not do, but that didn't mean they couldn't be a great help also.

It was obvious too that God was more grateful to the watchman than most. And why shouldn't he: he had business to take care of and a great responsibility for the people of God. A leader always needed assistance, and would amply reward those who helped him. The watchman would be well compensated up above in heaven for beating all kinds of crap out of the clerical students that he caught nearly in flagrante. But he wasn't certain that maybe the watchman mightn't slip in through the windows himself unbeknownst to anyone. How could he have the patience to be hanging around a harem like that all through the night, heretics and all as they were, without being tempted to give a little tap to a window?

I mean, it was well known that their type kept a ready reserve of gin stacked away in their rooms. He was an army man too. Strong as a champion ox. He knew *The Midnight Court*, whatever that was. A big healthy hero, the right man in the right place at the right time. Hands as big as windmills, legs like tree trunks, a crotch that could crush. He was all hands and legs and trunk. And, of course, he recited the *Court* to those women.

What more could be said? N. had his doubts. How did he know that he wasn't sneaking back from one of those women when he caught N.? It was hardly likely that the clerical students were half as bad. Couldn't it be that he was being tempted over there and into their rooms as a kind of favour, a benefit in kind? Or maybe, who knows, maybe it wasn't the clerical students who were beating a path to the window, but anybody at all whom he might let in? Who knows, maybe all that kindness was only a trick to get him to come back, hitch him up with a young one who would duly rob him? He was the spit and image of Simon. If it wasn't that the watchman was so tall and lanky you could never tell one from the other. He spouted twice as much bullshit about angels, no matter what else he was on about. But despite all of that, angels watching over him, holy winds from above, inspirations from God, he still couldn't find out who opened the lock. If he couldn't crack something as simple as that, was he in any position to offer N. any real help or any proper advice?

'May God forgive me!' N. exclaimed, 'imagine giving any credence to dirty thoughts like that about someone who has done so much for me.'

But N. could not entirely banish that unease in his gut. Oh yes, the watchman was another version of Simon, a kind of summary of him. Anybody who saw their faces, and nothing else, couldn't really tell them apart.

N. was particularly grateful to the watchman that he allowed him wash, shave, shite, and shampoo and the chance to do himself up. But there was still a kind of frivolity about him during that brief time, a frivolity that shone through just the way he was. It was hardly likely now that he would admit that he had slept with Squimzy last night, and that her scaly legs nearly made him throw up when he came to in the morning.

It began to come clear that Squimzy's legs weren't the problem at all, but his own state of mind. He had to recognize that this mental aberration was not something that started in his own mind, but a sickness that had its basis in his disgust with his own body, a sickness which emigrated from there into his mind. One of the girls in the office used to say that the immaterial body was only an outgrowth of material substance anyway, with just the shape of a body slapped on top of it. If that was true, then why wouldn't all that bodily filth just seep into his mind. After all, how did we know that the mind was in any way guilty of its own bad thoughts? Instead of running around praying, or going to confession, or to the mission, or to the Legion of Mary, maybe a body would be better off going for a swim, or taking a shower, or shaving himself, or scrubbing his teeth, doing whatever he had to and cleaning himself up after all that.

N. heard that women didn't have as many dirty thoughts as men did, and that nuns had the least of all. Nuns were always neat and tidy and scrubbed up clean. No doubt those thoughts were always entertained and enjoyed by those large-lubber lumps of Brothers most of the time! Maybe women paid more attention than men to bodily cleanliness. Men didn't give a shit. They'd spill booze or any kind of gunk on themselves, or they'd throw up on their clothes. It appeared to N. that if someone, by dint of massive effort, could keep his whole body clean of every spick and splotch all through his life, he would be very close to original innocence. But wouldn't this be even more difficult than avoiding sin? It would be a great opportunity for somebody working in an office. It would be easier for N. to avoid bodily dirt than for a druggie.

But then again, N. thought that this couldn't be right. He thought it was weird, given that he had just washed himself, that he should have such unworthy and nasty thoughts about the watchman. If he was really a bad guy, he certainly kept himself sparkling clean . . .

There was no decent hiding place in the church apart from the wall just behind the door. Wasn't it just as well? This was a place where he would hardly be noticed. His thoughts were weighing so heavily upon him that N. hardly noticed either the priest or the church. This was the same church he was in the night before and it was the same priest who said the Mass and had spoken to him. He was delivering one great booming blast of a sermon. N. was hoping that he would get some revelation about his own situation, some kind of guidance, an inspiration as clean and clear as the growing grass.

The watchman had surmised that that might not happen. Despite all this, it seemed that God favoured the watchman more than most. A person should be grateful for any kind of revelation, no matter how mean or minuscule. The worst thing about these revelations was that they could just as easily lead you astray as put you on the right path, you were just as likely to end up in the arms of a cop or in the embrace of a civil servant, given what the scattered mind could properly grasp. N. was often accused of being superstitious. One of these revelations had ordered him, not that long ago, to head straight for Squimzy just like that. It had led him also to entangle with the widow Waddel's wiles, for what that was worth. In that particular case the watchman would say that that idea didn't come from God at all, that he had ignored the very one God had given him. But neither the watchman's revelation of grace nor the widow's enticing fleshly vision was coming to him now . . .

Maybe N. didn't give himself time to take much notice of the sermon. The priest said that even if you destroyed the entire universe, but you had love and charity in your heart, you would be forgiven. 'Even if you rob the destitute and the down-and-outs, the poor and the rich, God will forgive you, if thou givest it away again as alms.' But how could the priest for all his wisdom know, N. was asking himself, if this was done whether it would be a travesty of justice, or justice in all its propriety carried through to the end? Maybe the person robbed would never get his stuff back, and be at the loss of it forever? N. had read that property and possessions were a means of perfecting and developing the person. Every increase in his wealth was also an addition to his personality. It didn't really matter whether this addition was for better or for worse. It was an addition, because it altered the person one way or another, made him go in a direction other than where he was now. Every robbery or swindle or theft was a darkening of the soul, a closing off of possibilities, a disorder in na-

ture, even if a full act of contrition and compensation and resolution of sinning no more was made. He himself, N., would never
get over the theft of his wallet, even if it happened that he got it
all back safe and sound. He would never know how his personality had been punctured, his sense of himself wounded these
past two days. If the story was ever told, he was sure it would be
entitled, as it should be: 'The two days my personality was dis-
placed.' Which reminded him of the course of his life all over
again . . .

But the priest was coming between him and everything else.
Wouldn't it have been great if the priest had condemned the robbery in the first place before anything else? How did anybody
know whether the guy who snatched his wallet mightn't give it
all away as a gift, as charity? He might dispense it generously to
corner boys hanging around, dossers on the dole, ladies of the
night, without he himself, the guy whom it belonged to, getting
a brass farthing or a copper cent. The thing was, if you were giving
to beggars, you could give to any one of them you liked. But
you'd think that a priest would have some sense of perspective
and would be more careful of what he was saying . . .

He was away in full throttle: 'Verily, it is said, you should
look after one another, there is no greater commandment. This
does not necessarily abrogate the saying that charity begins at
home. But it could be a sin against God's love for us all. You do
not suffer your neighbor to endure hunger or hardship. Give unto
him drink when he is thirsty, feed him when he is hungry, help
him on that day when tribulation or death darkeneth his door.

Death often cometh like unto a thief in the night. He careth not if the bereaved have not the price of the burial or the cost of the funeral . . .'

'The fucker,' N. muttered. A big lump of glug that was too thick for his windpipe rose up in his innards. He would shout out to the congregation that there wasn't enough of the love of God in his heart to give a pinch of snuff or a tincture of tobacco to a corpse for nothing . . .

'But always remember that the clergy are your neighbours also. Do not leave them go hungry or go without the goods of human kindness any more than you would anybody else of your neighbours. For, behold, to leave a neighbor hungry is not like unto leaving one of God's clergy hungry. To leave a member of the clergy go hungry is the same as leaving the Body of Christ, the Mystical Body go hungry . . .'

'Oh, the bad black fucker!' N. said, more loudly this time, contorting his whole body around so that you'd think that all his strength and vigour had gathered in his lips. His tongue slobbered and stuttered in his mouth. But then he ceased. He would give his answer in one of the evening newspapers. They would certainly publish his letter. He would sign himself *Fr. Reverend* or *Catholic and Proud of it* or something like that in a series of them. He'd find out what this particular priest's nickname was in the parish. If he inserted that quite subtly in the letter, he knew that the paper would never cop on to it. You can be quite sure he had a nickname, they all did, Tommy, Johnny Porridge, Michael the Mucker, Peggy's Leg, the Honorable Gimme Gimme, Dr.

Rich, Cod the Parish, Brian Bungut, Loopy Loudmouth, Slick Synnott . . . There was no point in answering him here and now. There was also the civil service and the television . . .

He recalled seeing a phosphorescent glow from the flotsam on the water when he was a small boy. He couldn't quite remember it clearly now, and maybe it was only a shimmering glister even on that particular night. He hadn't the least clue where that memory had come from, but it called his attention to the shaft of light that was coming in through the church window, a kind of innocent beam of sunlight that couldn't be trapped but had just wandered in, although it was quite clearly making itself known as a genuine integral part of all creation. It awoke a small glint of unexpected hope in N. He waited there through the next Mass, and the one after that, which happened to be the last one. But he had long given up paying any attention to what was going on around him.

Other images were flooding in from the back roads of the rivers of his memory that he had never much bothered about before. That bright summery day when he saw seven or eight heads of cattle lying down in the sun in pairs — cows that were kind of yellow with a white streak across their heads — their faces directly up against one another while they chewed the cud; he had no idea why this was such a wonderful scene that he could now recall it. A cow was a big beast. It took up four times as much space to stand on than a man. Maybe it was because they were that big that they were happy in themselves. It was difficult to make out what was going on behind the big moo eyes in a cow's mind, back there behind those big innocent stupid orbs. But it could also be that there was sweet fuck all, just nothing, not a bit. But on the other hand it could also be again that they were just about as innocent behind those big soft slobby peepers as that huckster of God's love above there on the altar behind the smooth grace of his hands, his gentle genial gestures, the way in which he would occasionally just slightly bestir himself that made him look like a cow about to start munching . . .

Just then N. felt the firm hand on his shoulder, a voice as if from above, like a trap snapping on him:

'You are not allowed to fall asleep in the church . . .'

It was the priest. As soon as he saw it was N., he changed utterly. N. immediately thought of clothes which had lost their softness, from which the natural freshness had gone. When N. got to look at him properly, all he could see was a patch of brightness, but a kind of dull brightness like the common unsparkling kind that half-shines from so-called bright things like the sacred garb of bishops, the uncertain grin of a cop, the bald patches of professors, the white wet feet of washerwomen wallowing in the water . . .

'You were here last night?' the priest said. 'Wasn't I talking to you out there the other evening? . . . I went and spoke after that to your parish priest, Father Matthew. A friendly man. He said that people had approached him about a burial . . . Monday, I think he said . . . I understood from him that everything was alright, fixed up, settled. You can go home now without any worries, no need to be ashamed, that is if you weren't home yet. Off you go now . . .'

He was being packed off from the church just as the manager packed him off from the department store yesterday! A bit like the way the shopkeeper huckster had treated him also. N. brought down the shutters, the only kind of defensive wall he had in his armoury. One of his cheeks was chattering charitably away with the priest, while his other cheek had turned into a fiery fury of anger and insult:

'Oh yes, I'll go home. Most certainly I'll toddle off home. Any chance though that you might slip me a loan, let's say at forty percent, or even more? I'd prefer that the profit would go to the Mystical Body than to some due boy foreign lender. I'd hate to see any trouble accruing to the Mystical Body.'

'I actually think that you should take off home now without delay like a good Christian before you are brought home in a way you will never forget. It simply is not good enough that a civil servant should be going around insulting people and trying to incite trouble or whatever on the streets while his wife . . .' The roughness bristled through his voice like the grunts of a wild boar. N. realized that he meant what he said.

While he was wandering through the streets he passed the pub, but there was neither sign nor signal of the Do-Gooder. N. headed off without quite knowing where he was going through old alleys, arches, and back lanes. If he ever wanted his help, the help of the Do-Gooder, he wanted it now. His problems were only beginning, if that was possible. He would prefer that nothing would be arranged when he got home, and that he, N., would have to fix everything up, even if it was just patchy and messy. If there was no doing without him at home, he would have to put up with it, just accept things as they were, suffer along and do whatever had to be done, however reluctantly, even put a cap on his own neglect and indifference. If the Mystical Body was to be believed, certain things were already ordained. It was most likely that other things were ordained and arranged in just the same way. He would only now be like the negligent neighbor, the default dumb bunny who turns up when the cow has been hauled out of the hole long before then . . .

She was going to be buried on Monday or Tuesday. His colleagues in the civil service would know about it, those who didn't know it already. They would come to the funeral. He had no real claim on them. They were all good harmless plodders, as many civil servants were. They were well used to being damned if they did and dumbned if they didn't. They had their own system for distributing praise and reward according to the values of the civil service; this usually depended on one's value, salary, standing, allowances, and how close one was to the next little step on the promotion ladder. It was often mumbled that this was the only bit that was left of genuine Irish customs in the civil service. They would be at the funeral simply because it was the right thing to do according to the system of rank and reward which dominated their thinking. The greatest insult would be if he wasn't there himself, especially as they were going to be there simply to pay him their respects. It would be a terrible disgrace if some Top Notch in the civil service was going around on such an occasion without some junior hack hanging out of him and hugging his shadow.

N. had burned his boats and sunk his ships a long time ago as regards his reputation in the civil service. They would be very sorry for his troubles, of course, be deeply sorry for the death of his wife, but then again, they could be easily pissed off and not very understanding when he stayed out for a part of the day to look after her. He was often absent since she got the bad news. Maybe too often. This he would never know unless a promotion was in the offing.

He was owed some compassionate leave because of her death. Officially, of course, he wouldn't have to explain in the office what happened, why he wasn't at work, or even at the funeral. But there was an unwritten rule, a fundamental understanding that was really only a plethora of precedents. According to the culture of the civil service, it was a kind of an insult not to ask someone like N. what happened to him exactly. It might even have to be put to him more precisely with all the gory details intact, and how exactly it affected him, all this and more so that his reputation would not be sullied. If it happened that he didn't reveal all, or did so reluctantly, or not the whole naked truth, this was a much greater crime against civility than any other charge that could be conjured up.

More than that, it would be seen in even a worse light because it was something that didn't directly affect him in his position as a civil servant. Because by definition, a civil servant was a civil servant in body and in mind, whole and complete. No other bit of him was anything other than a civil servant, except insofar as it might in exceptional circumstances be allowed as a privilege for the purposes of convenience according to law that he could perform duties as another person who was for the time being not a civil servant for the present. Inasmuch as someone was a civil servant he was an official being and the essence and foundation of his life were the rules of the civil service. In that case, it might be surmised that the rules could sometimes be broken, or avoided, or got around, or twisted, or bent, or softened, or reinterpreted, or misinterpreted, or even totally dumped if you could get away with it. This was recognized within certain strict and accepted guidelines, as was common knowledge in the civil service.

But no rules were ever written for the liminal personality, the person on the edge, that member of the civil service who had permission now and again, on and off, in some places, for certain purposes, to act as if he wasn't a civil servant at all at that time, to act in a different way for those ends at that particular time. They were a lot more severe, more dictatorial, more civil servantistical, more official about issues on the outer limits, about a semi-detached peninsula like that which was beyond the bounds of the rules, than there were about a question that was within the remit of the civil service without fear or favour or doubt or debate. N. knew well that he would have to give an account of his stewardship out in those areas sometime.

He knew that a crime against the civil service was in itself a breach of the laws of the country. That undoubtedly meant that a civil servant could not in any circumstances break the laws in public he had made himself. There were so many rules that were a crime in the service although they weren't a crime according to the laws of the country. In reality, nobody knew what a crime was and what wasn't in that peninsular and crepuscular world. Nobody knew what a crime was until it was committed. It was only then that a crime was assessed as such. N. could spend the whole day in the office twiddling his thumbs. But if he did the same thing while standing at a street corner and this was officially known, then that was the end of his chances of promotion forever and ever. In fact, it was much more likely that he would be demoted or even drummed out of the service on some grubby measly pension years before his time. N. knew of one colleague who had spent forty years in a civil service office during which time he did nothing apart from scratching the top of his head. He read the paper every morning. Then he would clean and prepare the top of his pen and set it down in precisely the same spot on his desk before he started scratching. One of his superiors in the civil service caught him at lunch time in a public park not too far away doing the same thing. He sent instructions that he be summoned to his office that afternoon:

'Why were you scratching your head on a park bench in a public place?'

'The way it is,' he said, 'it's a habit I happen to have developed in the office for the last forty years. There are so many problems I encounter in my work as a civil servant that we have no way of solving, at least in the short term. I often thought that they were there just inside my skull, like a kind of worm, and I thought if I rattled my head up and down and rocked and rolled it that it would shake it up and shake it out. As you can see, my good man, every single wisp and stray strand of my hair has been worn away by now, and the top of my head has been scraped away to nearly nothing so that I don't have to worry about all the crap that happened to me years ago any more. That actually means that I have more time and leisure to think about the work of the civil service.'

'Your conscientiousness with regard to your duties is well noted,' his boss said, 'and I certainly hope that you will not cease in your determination to fulfill the duties of the office, but I must warn you that you cannot display your internal loyalty in such a public manner. In the first instance it cannot be admitted that there is a problem which the civil service has not solved. And thus, a problem solved is not a problem at all. And because every problem is completely dealt with as soon as it arises, it follows that there is no further problem for the civil service to address. This kind of thing has happened already, make sure you note it well. The accused was only just about within two years of getting his pension. The minister wrote to him. The fact that the minister wrote to him was proof positive that he had never heard of the case. The minister informed him that he was certain that the minister was of the definite opinion that such extramural activity of this nature was greatly detrimental to the administrative affairs of the state, and if there was a further occurrence that the minister would not be indisposed to examining the transgression in a more serious light.'

N. was well aware that what he had done could be looked at in a much more serious light, and especially because he had not transgressed any particular rule that could be referenced. He would have to make up some story. The simpler the story the more likely it would be believed because it would have the ring of truth about it. One simple unified story, one direct narrative, one tale for all and all for one. He recalled the excuse he had concocted for his wife's sisters yesterday about the reason for his delay. That would do the business just as well for those in the office also, except that he had added that he was knocked down by a car and lost his memory. He would have to add that it all happened after he was robbed. The office crowd would have some contact with the cops anyway, and would have heard about the robbery. That would have added another ring of truth to the mix. He wouldn't be in his right mind having been robbed. Civil servants were a notoriously nosy sort casting a pall of doubt down from the heights of their own Mount Sinai on the underlings who crapped and crept and crawled below. He would have to tell them which hospital he was in and they wouldn't rest easy until they had searched it out and rung it up, given their own sense as the official pack hounds of the state. They would ask when the case about his accident would be brought before the courts.

If he said he had come to a private settlement with the guy who knocked him down, they would insist on finding out how much he was awarded, and maybe even expect that he'd spread a bit of it around. Somebody would hear something about his shenanigans on the bog that Saturday afternoon. He could, of course, pretend that he was sick at home, or flattened by a bout of depression in the hospital, or in some nursing home. One of them would try to search him out until they'd find him, touch him with a doubting finger, measure him for his height, or the way he stood, or his weight, assess his lack of intelligence compared to theirs, and then pronounce: 'This indeed is the civil servant N., in this particular time and space, with all his faculties.'

It was too true that any dereliction of duty on the part of a civil servant was a dereliction of his own better interests, and he was duty bound to investigate the mysterious borders and frontiers and outer limits of his fellow civil servants, to dispel the fairy fog of uncertainty by clearing his own way through it. There was always danger in the illusion and ignorance of another's personality: he might seem to be just a passing distant star sweeping by in the anonymous night, but before you knew it, there he was as an immovable object grinning down on you from a higher rung on the ladder . . .

N. started inventing twenty different stories without being able to finish any one of them to his satisfaction, and he just dumped them to one side as his mind got tired of trying to pin them down. What would happen if he bumped into one of these civil servants on the street and got asked about the SOS? He knew full well that this SOS was going to haunt him for the rest of his official days. As long as it remained unexplained it would always be the subject of some urgent serious investigation in the civil service. Everything in the civil service was an investigation, every single one as serious and as urgent as the next, on whose resolution the prosperity of the state depended, not to say its very existence. N. knew full well that he was the chaff in the midst of the rich crop of wheat. This guilt led him despite himself in off the road to a narrow opening where four different garages stood before him.

N. knew he was a marked man. His fate could be decided — a soft sly silken query from the mouth of a false friend — it could jump out at him from anywhere. Where was there any refuge? He thought of Squimzy. Should he call her? She wouldn't be up yet. She wouldn't hear him. She would be whacked out in a deep sleep in the morning. He didn't have her number. The whole confusion had driven it out of his head. It was in his other suit at home. It wasn't in the book, and yet half the city had it. Anyway, there wasn't much point. She had made her own use of him last night. She'd have another sucker today.

This in itself made him sad. He had to admit to himself that it was a kind of abstract sadness, metaphysical almost. There couldn't be any real definite sadness or sorrow, or it could be there only in a theoretical way. He had to presume that whatever prevented her from taking up with other men was what prevented her taking up with him also. Part of Squimzy's attraction, part of her magic, was that she'd shag any man she fancied without having a preference for one rather than another. In that way her experience with the lot of them was a kind of a favour which she granted to the man she was shagging at any particular time. Not only was she, Squimzy, giving herself to that guy, but she was also bestowing a gift of all the other men of whom she knew something of the secret recesses of their hearts. Sometimes Colm gave her short shrift or even worse. But despite this she liked the work. Part of its attraction was that it gave her the opportunity to ride a different man every night if she wished . . .

From the top of one of the garages a bird deposited a yellow squishy shit down on N.'s back, but he didn't notice it. He was trying to think of other hiding places, or shelters. The sourpuss in the bookie's yesterday? Forget that for a start. The whore in the public park? Forget that one too. The wide widow Waddel? A woman wanting a hard squeeze from a horny man as much as anyone around the town. It mightn't be a bad place to go. But then N. started thinking about the things he would rather squeeze. A press bought secondhand, a heater which you had got on the cheap! She'd probably see the death in the paper in the morning. Then she'd come to the house. 'Just like our own John went exactly,' she'd say. 'I hurried out to the kitchen to make a cup of tea. Just for one minute! I was only just back when he left out a little gasp and he was gone, gone just like that, without a word, without a whisper, without a goodbye . . .'

If she came to the house N. knew that he would have to handle her, so to speak. There would be a strong smell of scallions from her breath, she'd be lumpy, bumpy, sticky, bristly in all her parts as if pigs' heads were stuffed under her clothes, slithering and sliding out of his embrace because her slippers were flapping and falling off her feet. And the same natter, 'He was gone, gone just like that . . .'

Despite himself, N. found himself wandering back along the well-trodden path of his old thoughts. What was the first, the most urgent thing he had to do? The grave, the coffin, the undertaker, which was it? The grave wasn't needed unless there was a coffin to go into it. A coffin required a corpse. If the corpse was to be disposed of there had to be an undertaker. Or maybe the whole thing should be the other way round. There would be no need for an undertaker if there wasn't a body in the first place. Therefore, this was the way it went: undertaker, corpse, coffin, grave. Oh, no it wasn't, it was: corpse, undertaker, coffin, grave.

N. imagined the four garages as a kind of a square and he set them down in this order: the corpse on the bottom left-hand side, and then moving around clockwise to the undertaker, the coffin above that and on back returning to the grave at the end. This arrangement satisfied him, all the way from the corpse to the undertaker, from thence to the coffin, and on to the grave, this was N.'s reasoning. It seemed to him to be the only essential order of things, since death came as part of the lottery of life. It had to be that you would be contravening some basic law of existence any other way, despite the fact that you could go from corpse to grave to coffin to undertaker, or despite that you could go from corpse to grave or from undertaker to corpse. Or you could simply change the corners around and keep going on the same way without cease. It suddenly began to dawn on N. that with all his messing about and ins and outs and ups and downs that he had only managed to dig a big square hole which he was in danger of falling into himself if he spent any longer staring at the problem . . .

All the same the grave itself was there, or if it wasn't it should be. How she would be brought there was only a matter of detail, of convention. That had to be the case as there was, after all, a body. If anything was at all certain it was the body, that body, that corpse that was the cause of all the worry and all the concern. It was hard to believe that something as heavy, as leaden, unfeeling, breathquenched as a corpse could raise up such a whirlwind of worry, could ensnare the living in such a trap of responsibility. The corpse was there: that was it, couldn't be denied. But this wasn't the first time there was a corpse, it had happened many times before without all these extra hanging-out dangly supplemental extra bits: the undertaker, the coffin, even a grave. A corpse was a fine normal thing. But what about all those other parasites and ghoulsuckers feeding on the business of having to deal with it? Shouldn't it be that all these other things would be an afterthought which the corpse would be able to deal with automatically, if there being a corpse there in the first place was really necessary? In this case the corpse itself was more like the afterthought, an incidental result of all these other things, far more important and fundamental than he being at the centre of the story. Some spanner had been chucked into the works . . .

He could readily see that this kind of thinking was another dead end with a wall of confusion bringing up its rear. Instead of

beginning with the raw material, the corpse, maybe he should re-
wind back from the end, the very last thing. Start with the cemetery, with the grave. Or even to jump forward in time and begin
with the vault. The vault derived from the grave, from a closed
grave. The grave was open because a coffin had to go down into
it. The coffin was to go into it because it contained a corpse, or
should do, before it was closed, that is, to make a closed coffin out
of an open one before it went into the grave. There was a corpse
in it, the remains of a live person, and the live person . . . N. got a
grip on himself. He was repeating the childish story of Tweedle-
dum and Tweedledee again. This same old waffly nonsense was a
kind of perverse compensation for his own inadequacies. There
were other ways of repeating the same story. There were many
other things you could do with a body besides sticking it in a coffin and other things that could be done to a coffin besides sticking it into a hole in the ground. Send it floating down the river,
for example. Leave it overnight at the closed door of a church, or
in a public garden, or on the roof of Simon's garage, or outside
the front door of someone who was trying to get promotion before you. Not to mention that it could be stuck into the bin or
burned to a frazzle in the back garden. It was against social convention and the dictates of good manners that a coffin would appear in any place without a corpse to be placed in it at the same
time. If something without precedence like that should ever take
place, a corpse would have to be provided, or obtained, for the
coffin. Nobody had ever heard of a coffin wandering about by

itself for more than three or four days. There was always work or business to be done for a coffin. The opposite would be of the same order of horror as the ghostly hearse, the headless body or the phantom bier. N. thought if that was to happen they would have to declare a national day of prayer . . .

That was the first necessity: to get a body to put into the box; then to set about negotiating with an undertaker to do all those things to get it to the cemetery, delegating some of his duties to the corporation workers and others. According to all the rules, precedents, and conventions that were commonly accepted, not one link in this chain could be skipped or passed over from one to another. You fulfill your own functions with solemn perfection as is only right and proper for a solemn function. Neither an undertaker nor the driver of a ghostly hearse could ever handle a spade to open or to close a grave . . .

It brought a certain peace to N.'s mind that that was it, he had it completely from top to bottom and from bottom to top. From his initial premise that there existed both a vault and a grave, he had proved without a shadow of doubt that there had to be a corpse also! . . .

But then, a big black cloud of doubt like a war goddess from on high descended on him. Was there really a body? How did he know for certain that there was a body? Wouldn't it have been very easy for the ugly sisters to spread the rumour and to make sure it reached his ears just to give him grief and see how he re-acted. They could always say after that that they thought she had died. And how did they know that she hadn't. He hadn't made any arrangement with a doctor to pay her a daily visit. It would have cost a fortune!

Certainly, the Mystical Body had told him what his parish priest had said, or thought he said. Thought he said was right, of course, but N. presumed at the time that it was the whole unvarnished truth. How could he tell that it wasn't some other body the parish priest was talking about, somebody with the same surname? It might all have been in his eyes, the parish priest was so used to seeing corpses coming in and out and coming and going all times of the day and night, even looking forward to them. N. couldn't remember if he had given his name to the Mystical Body. There was a large population in the parish. Funerals were as common and as regular as waves on the shore. Maybe the parish priest was not talking about any funeral at all, not a particular one. He was more or less deaf, except when it came to counting money. N. thought it was time to buy a newspaper . . .

That would solve everything, if there was no corpse, if she was still alive. I certainly hope so, he said. If the corpse simply melted away that was the end of all the bother about the coffin, the undertaker, the grave, that huge cold lumpy weight of responsibility lifted off him so that he could walk lightsome again on the new soft sward after being wrapped so long in the straitjacket of uncertainty . . .

There was a man on the bridge reading a newspaper. N. asked him could he take a gander at the death notices. If he could have changed his mind he would have done so immediately. Far better to have the worm of doubt gnawing at your gut than to have exact knowledge, the knowledge that destroys. His hands were shaking uncontrollably. Was there really a body, and if there was? . . . But supposing there wasn't? His eyes spun around in a wild whirl. They took over all his faculties, his reason, his horror, his hands, his head, his heart . . .

'What's up with you?' the paper man asked, stretching out his hand to get it back.

'The body,' N. said, flatly.

'The body!' the man exclaimed.

'Yes,' N. said. 'It will be brought to the church this evening and the burial will be in Kilnamanagh at twelve o' clock. There is a body there after all . . .'

The man left him totally puzzled. N. gripped the rail of the bridge. This was the whole responsibility business cast down before him again like a field of skulls. There was no escape now, and the time was so short. If there was one sensible sober person he could bring with him to the house, he could act as an intermediary. At least he would be able to soften or deflect the worst of the blows that were destined to rain down on him. He thought again about Simon and the rest of the gang who were in the pub yesterday. He knew where they lived and had some of their telephone numbers. He'd have to get around their women and their wives, of course. Women were very quick to blame somebody like N. who went missing without ever asking why he might have gone missing in the first place. Women were always suspicious of men. They firmly believed that it was always other women who kept them away from the family Rosary. They loved to think that their own men were paragons of virtue, or they would be if it wasn't for the bad example of people like N., and the kind of rubbishy shite he spouted . . .

N. knew far too much about the men himself. They never needed any persuading to get him to visit them. They'd help him along and with sweet talk and some persuasive palaver, most people shut up and listened. That's when they'd change their tune, just like a long stretch of road going off plainly into the distance, but which then suddenly turned into a treacherous byway. All good fun and chatty jokiness, of course. They could tell more lies with the twist of a mocking grin than someone else could by swearing on the truth of the Bible. They would put lies, damned lies, and mendacious stories into N.'s mouth, making up things that were supposed to have happened to him:

'Did you hear that N. was trying to get a cut on the price of the coffin down in Lonergan's? But then he was robbed. There was this woman came out of the backstreet and robbed him . . . A woman met him under Gobbler's Arch said she'd introduce him to a cheapskate undertaker who'd do it for next to nothing and take him back home here too. Laid a hand—entirely by accident,' this other one said—'on his conker bonker and that's *Dainty's Dream* . . .'

They'd burst their holes laughing at N. trying to wriggle out of these stories:

'You'd think with that mug on you, N., that we had it in for you or something . . . Are you telling us you don't have a conker bonker? . . . Shit happens, accidents happen all the time. It could happen to a parish priest, although mind you, I never heard it happening to a priest here in this parish . . .'

That's the way they were. They couldn't help it. Their wives would love to believe—and they knew full well they would love to believe—that there were people out there much worse than their own husbands. As the story was being told, the women would scrunch their faces up into balls of disgust while looking at N. With all the effort and mumbling put into denying what they were saying, N. would contradict and trip himself up. This limp and wimpy defence was even worse than if he never tried to speak up for himself. There could be somebody there who got so incensed and flew into a paroxysm of rage that he might clatter N. in the face, or maybe even half-kill him . . .

It had finally dawned on N., but not for the first time, that he was like a dog howling at the moon while whistling in the dark. It would make far more sense, he said to himself, and he hoped for the last time, to leave all the arrangements for the funeral and the burial to those at home who had already done that, or so it would appear. They knew best. The dead person was there with them in their presence like arrears that had to be paid. They'll arrange the burial, anyway. If I went home now, I'd only put them all off. N. felt that he was the match in a kindling of anger that would require only the slightest puff to set the whole lot ablaze. Who knows that he mightn't be the reason for them having another corpse on their hands? . . .

This idea gave birth to another great feeling of liberation. He had drawn the poison! He thought back on these past few months in which they had caused him to suffer, on the crush of worry and endless torture they had inflicted on him. Trying to explain to the civil service why he was absent. Trying to dress the sour truth up in a sweet acceptable sauce of excuse. A waste of time, all of it, what else? They would far sooner swallow some cock and bull story, a pack of plausible lies that could be peddled by dickying it up in a web of rules and precedents, than the straight raw and rough but ready truth out of God's own mouth . . .

N. had only now been released from the horror of the harrow on which he had been stretched for months, and especially these past few days. He was beginning already to enjoy the day. He was left entirely to his own devices without any thing to do, without any thing to take care of. His wife would be buried despite him, without his help, without the necessary torrent of tears. His relations would be relieved that he wasn't there. She wouldn't be buried in peace and with propriety even if he was to turn up now when he wasn't wanted. Him being there would only spell disaster and trouble and strife. And even if this wasn't so, it would only seem to N. that he didn't really give much of a damn . . .

Like as if he was testing this new liberation in his limbs, N. strode out with a lively step, bouncing along like a youngfella at a local dance, and sat himself down on the grassy knoll beside the canal. He could feel his mind and his tongue as liberated as his limbs. If any nosy civil servant happened to pass by he knew full well up front what he would say to him:

'An undertaker and a coffin equals a grave. An undertaker

plus a coffin plus a grave minus a corpse is an unknown quantity. An unknown quantity squared is disorder, anarchy, the beginning of the end, the trumpet of judgment day. The Antichrist is associated with the Queen of Country. A new country ballad made her surrender to the Antichrist . . .'

This was liberation unbound for N. He would keep on repeating those words to himself all day and keep nothing else in his head. The civil servant could think whatever he liked for as long as he liked, even that he was completely off his rocker, and even nuts. Even the crazy entertaining pantomime that was the civil service couldn't get much fun or satisfaction from someone whose wife had just died, and he was robbed, and was totally confused for now even though he might be able to clear it up in good time . . .

The police weren't pissing him off much either. He'd say to them that he wasn't trying to go home, that he wouldn't go home, that there wasn't a thing or a tittle in the law that would force him to go home, that he was his own master, that he knew what he was doing, that he knew what to say and how to say it, he was somebody who spoke to the people of Ireland every week, or regularly, sometimes. If he had done anything wrong, arrest him and charge him and that's it. That was the way . . .

The day awoke. Gaudy butterflies were flitting between the water and the bank. Two sailors from the American ship that was in the port for the past few days sat down on the seat beside him. This was mainly because of the high-pitched giggling of two young women who were there just hanging out near them. Some people had no sense of what was proper. But this had nothing to do with being proper. They wanted a man after midnight, and these two might do just nicely. Where was the woman, or maybe the man, whom these sun-burnished men from South America, maybe from Valparaiso itself, whose ship had furled its sails in this harbor and who brought the brightness of the sun and the promise of El Dorado printed on their uniforms to the dull and dun streets of this city, where was she, or he, who wouldn't be tempted to be blown away?

N. dozed into a long sleep. When he came to, one of the other American sailors noticed him at the end of the bench. His face grinned back at him like a welcome to his world, smiling like he was an ambassador to everybody and bidding best wishes to all who were around. His face shone like gold and stars sparkled in the depths of his eyes. He wasn't chewing his gums or spitting out gobs of mucky glob like the other two.

'You were out for the count there,' he said to N. who thought that the sweetness of his voice matched the kindness in his face. 'You didn't get much of a sleep last night, then?'

'A bit here and there.'

'Just like me, I'm telling you, just like me. But unfortunately, I went to sleep at the wrong time . . . A woman robbed me, every bloody red cent I had in my possession. She was knocking one of the crew and she took off with my pants and with all my money . . . I was too scuttered and blotto to notice it. Too fucking bad for me and for every other piss artist like me! I have one cunt of a hangover, and if a cent would cure it, I don't have it. Every man to his own woman,' he said, glancing over to the other seat, 'but the worst of all is to have sweet fuck all, and your pants gone to top it all. I've had it with women after last night. But I think I could drink the river dry today . . .'

While N. was listening to the sailor spinning out his tale of woe, he couldn't but help thinking that he was doing the telling, but then he commenced to build up the other's misfortune with beams and rafters of his own construction. Before long the sailor knew all about his wife's death and about Squimzy.

'Another hard man! After my own heart! So it goes, comrade!' his face transferring shiny doubloons of gold across to N.

N. liked the fact that he called him 'comrade.' N. was soon making it up to him. N. had accepted that this guy was a real comrade, unlike those he had been messing around with yesterday, neither the television crowd or Squimzy, nor the watchmen, nor anybody else apart from the Do-Gooder. N. told him all about that, the whole story.

'I know the way it is,' the sailor said, 'there are so many weird and wonderful things in this here country, leprechauns who have purses of gold and so on. I'd love to meet up with one of them today! We'd drink the pub dry! My father and my Uncle Peter, my Aunt Bridie, and the whole gang of Irish in Boston are always going on like that.'

'You're from Boston?' N. queried, and suddenly his interest flowed like a deer in a rushing stream—'

'Yep, from Boston, and we're heading back there straight away just after this.'

'I have two brothers and a sister, and three uncles in Boston.'

'Who are they? . . . Where exactly do they live? . . . I can't say I know them. But why would I? There are more Irish in Boston than in any town here in Ireland . . .'

They had a great chat about all of this. While they were gabbling away N. couldn't quite grasp the myriad of memories and moments that was bubbling up from the surging surf and in the forgotten dawns of his head, nor could he even manage to put them in any passable sequence. Squimzy and the night walker and the puss bitch with the tight arse and Simon and the whole lot of them belonged to when he was hemmed in like a serf slave. This man was a symbol of his liberation, like somebody who had just been created especially for this occasion, as new, as clean, as freshly minted as a silver coin on its birthday, or a new suit walking out from the bespoke tailor. N. recognized that here was a man who would never stinge on his sympathy, unlike most of the people he knew. Despite the little bitty time they had spent together, N. thought that he had opened up, however faintly, a vein of humanity, friendship, and camaraderie that never would be found outside of fantasy literature.

He had opened up a rare soft spot in N. himself. It never dawned on him that his decision not to go home had anything to do with this. It was all down to the kindness and humanity of this sailor, of this he was certain. He offered to buy him a drink. He did this mechanically as a sign of gratitude, without thinking, without knowing if he still had the price of a drink at all, or not. Anyway, they'd mosey down to Sweeney's pub, he was known there and he'd get a few drinks on the tab, on the never never. Sweeney knew he was often on the radio and on the television. Sweeney would also more than likely have seen the death notice in the paper. No publican would ever be shocked that those in a funeral party or relatives of the dead would get a few drinks on credit. N. was gagging for a drink.

'We'll tell them,' N. said, 'we'll tell them in this pub that we're related and that you came to visit me. My name is N., you can call me N. What's it your name is? . . . Great, brilliant, that's it, Ed!'

N. never felt himself so free, so fulfilled, so much at home with his person and his body as he looked, as he was then, all the way through and down. He belonged to himself, every tiny weeny weeshy bit of him! He couldn't sense any little bit of others' humanity, not friends, not relations, not fellow workers trying to muscle in on him, no sense of anybody else's frost cooling his personality, none of their clouds darkening his skies, nobody trying to trip him up on the path he had laid out for himself. Neither Simon nor Larry could finish a drink without taking the piss. Colm was alright when you got him on his own. But he always saw people as a kind of picture, even a photograph. The closest he ever got to humanity was to imagine a photo as a person just so long as it took him to fulfill his temporary function as a person. Then he would revert perfectly to that static standing which was his wont, his genuine fixed position, that of a photograph.

The civil service only ever saw people as already embalmed

precedents. N. got the impression that Ed saw people as people, and not as things or objects. He was his own yardstick for judging everybody else, but that stick could turn into a magic wand and turn all else out there into others of the same cut and of the same cloth. It might just be that N. could be his comrade and be entirely independent at the same time. His face might well be foreign, his eye lazy, his conversation kind and engaging letting him know that he was a comforting creature, last night's comforting creature come back again, but in a different form. That comforting creature took many shapes and forms, N. thought, and he had no intention forgetting that he might return.

N. was already thinking that Ed wasn't really from Boston, or even from America, or from anywhere else either. A comforting creature didn't have to be from any one particular place. But because of what Ed had already said about Boston he had started imagining that they had a special relationship, that they were both cursed because of their joint nature which explained their disaster with women the previous night, along with the fact that their wallets were robbed. Very soon he wouldn't find it easy to access his life before the time that he met Ed. His own life, and that of this other guy from the lands of sun and sand and sex and so-it-goes were two shadows slanting across one another. They complemented each other, one to one. Neither of them was complete on his own. It was like as if they were merging the sun, their strength, the sea, companionship, community, conversation, desperation, darkness, deviousness, wonder, welcome, and well-being all together. That ship that came from Valparaiso last night was indeed prophetic. What he was going to write about would be better now. Start somewhere else, then go off in a different direction: begin with this wonderful sailor whom he met on the streets of the city. He would follow him down to the harbor, the wonderful harbor of dreams, all the way down to the wonderful ship . . . His own life from now on would be a tale of wonder and expectation also.

The images in N.'s head, or the images that were entirely his own, were as lively and swift as a galloping racehorse by the time he got to the pub. He'd far prefer to start writing now than to go for a drink. Sweeney knew that his wife had died. He extended his sympathies. He asked him what he could get him. Of course, he'd get anything he liked on the tab. He could fix it up later. This made N. think bitterly again about the robbery, but he didn't say anything about this to Sweeney.

The sailor waved his hands about in big generous gestures and kept nodding his head every time he sought to thank N. properly.

'We'll have another day yet, even in this here town,' he said, trying to straighten out his mixed way of talking into one plain statement, 'but I'd much prefer if we had it in Boston. I'm telling you now, we're not likely to be robbed there.' N. had to pop one of his fingers to his lips as a kind of warning. The first thing Ed would do when he landed in Boston was to visit N.'s relations and tell them that he met big-hearted N. in Ireland and that he sent them all his best wishes, as huge as Ireland itself, and all his kindest regards to every single one of them and that the wonderful kind soul himself would be following him soon with his own greetings and blessings.

'It won't be that long anyway,' N. said, 'tell my uncle Willie . . .'

'Why would it be long? What's stopping you? . . . Lack of money, of dosh? You can't be kidding me! . . . The best way to get your money back, the money that was stolen, is to pay a visit to the States. You'll get ten dollars from everyone you meet. After one week you won't be out of pocket . . . Aren't I telling you you won't? But I'm telling you my good buddy, your Irish priests are destroying the country! Running around making the best of every opportunity and using every trick in the book. Organizing dances. They'd organize a dance for you too. Every man jack of them giving in an envelope at the door, and every one of them bursting at the seams with dollars. Not a wet cent less than thirty dollars in every one of them, comrade! . . . Priests? What else, but stuffed down in their own pockets. Their pockets bulging with enough to be stashed away. They say over yonder that every priest sends enough cash home to his brother so he can open a pub and sell whiskey at twice the price to Yanks during the summer . . . But what would delay you anyway, N.? You won't need any money. I'll be sailing away just after this later tonight and I'll bring you over, no problem . . . The law? No Irishman was ever afraid of the law. They spend their lives bribing them all the time in America . . . If you start imagining the worst like you are doing they'll soon nab you. I know some Irish guys who have been in the States for forty years who came in through Canada, all illegal, but they've never been caught yet. Now, comrade, do you feel any better? Listen, my good friend, my best pal, won't you be staying with your relations? You don't think your relations would shop you in, do you? . . . Ah, come on, come off it, there are many ways the cops can be bought!'

'Tell me about it,' N. said, as whatever doubts remained in his head that this fellow was really his lucky helpmate were banished. Every single thing he said only reinforced everything he had ever heard. He saw people returning from visiting their relations in the States and coming back with their pockets jingling with money. He could feel the urge for some of the same surging through him like the full tide. It was great if he could be brought over totally free of charge. At the same time a small pulse of worry kept tapping. Soon the booze that himself and Ed were downing would make its mark. This was the key that would release him from his imprisonment. To vanish for a while until they began to think he was dead, that he fell into the river that time his wife died, that his was the unrecognizable body that was found, that he drowned himself during those awful days! He'd be forgotten quickly enough. Very soon there wouldn't be even a glimmer of memory that he had ever drawn a breath. In the meantime, he'd have a brilliant holiday, his relations would splash out on him, ply him with drink, stuff his pockets with dollars. It was fantastic to think that even a fraction of this could be true! . . .

When he'd return they'd believe the rumour he had spread that he had lost his memory. Everybody would be reluctant to be too hard on him, to try and get him to cough up for his debts, half afraid about his sudden return. The death, the corpse, the coffin, the grave, they'd all vanish from his life like a wisp of smoke. That would be end of them, that would be that! . . .

N. thought that the barman might get a bit suspicious if he hung about too long while the corpse was laid out at home. It was getting late. He bought two bottles of whiskey for the funeral. These two bottles were like wrack floating around in his head since yesterday. Even now he needed the sailor's guiding hand on his elbow just to be sure that these bottles were not destined for the funeral . . .

As they were waltzing down through the streets the sailor struck up a song from some drama he had been in while he was in high school; he and it were telling N. about all the great places— wonderful magical places, N. thought—he had been: the sun-kissed kingdoms, the exotic countries, the flashy cities where he had visited; the tall model women, the small *petite* ones, the big-busted arse-bursting black broads; the yellow ones . . . just as if some wizard had stolen a handful of sunbeams and made them into celestial bouquets into which he had blown the breath of life. Their form had preceded their very life. The strength and warmth and mystery of those Oriental women . . .

'Squimzy's bone-white shanks,' N. said, and gave a silent shiver.

'. . . Nothing would ever best them except the cold, the cold of the weather, the deep cold of the heart . . .'

'But of course, there are no women like that in Boston?'

N. said, and who couldn't imagine any other place on earth in which his friends and relations were spending the sweat of their brow to be an anthology in which every poem was a beautiful woman of any colour you fancied.

'Oh, but there are, of course! Every kind of woman under the rainbow is in Boston. You'd see some of the finest things in America there, women of Irish descent, Germans, Spics, Chinks. I'm the right dumbass dodo that I didn't go back there. The drink, probably . . .'

'The drink is bad alright,' N. said. 'If I ever go to America, I won't touch a drop . . .'

'But why wouldn't you when you can get it, buckets of it, for nothing . . .'

The very phrase 'for nothing' gave N. a lift. The phrase reconstituted itself as a big beautiful Christmas present with all the dreams and memories which that entailed. N. recognized the lucky helpmate, one big Santa Claus spreading money around without even asking for it, a free lunch and lunches, bottles of whiskey, coffins, hearses . . . shops and stores and banks and pubs opened up before him overflowing with all unimaginable manner of goodies. There was no robbery, there was no need. America was the only place where that vision could come true. N. had no doubt that most things were as free as the wind—for people at any rate—there in America. This very specific thought, that there was a place out there where things could be got for nothing, peaked up his courage, strengthened his humanity, and injected his personality with hope. It banished once and for all the depressing despair which had haunted him about undertakers, coffins, and corpses, and the rest of it . . .

'. . . And then when you had enough on board to head off down to the beach, in her car, of course—everyone has a car in America—and stretch out there with her from top to tuft in a hollow of the hot sand . . . totally nudo bollocko. You'd have no need for any clothes, apart from maybe a slip of a sliver of something . . . Ah, come on out of that, have a bit of sense! Who would rob you? America is crawling with cops, not like this joint. One of them could be standing there right next to you in the middle of . . .'

'Looking at the two of us,' N. said, 'in our hot ash pelts? I'm not sure I'd like that. Will he be starko naked too?'

'Ah, cop yourself on, who would be looking at you? Small chance. He'd be minding his own business. And why would one of the fuzz be totally naked anyway? How else would you know a pig except by his clothes? But if you prefer, there's always doing it indoors . . . For someone as knowledgeable as you you're scared out of your pants about being robbed. I never came across any place apart from here where your trousers could be swiped . . . There are tons of women in America, hordes I said, believe me, no word of a lie. Most Yanks have two or three . . .'

'I'm not sure I'd fancy that either. That's the way Squimzy is. Every jockey on the dole couldn't service her if they got the chance, the ride!'

Even though there were lots of things he didn't like about

the States, he was convinced that it was the only place where things could be got for absolutely nothing.

They crumpled themselves in behind the shelter of a wall on the quay just outside a streetlamp that cast a pale light which was not unlike Squimzy's shanks in colour. The sailor made a wide gesture towards the world, one which looked like it had been made before.

'No need to be afraid, N. I'll look after you. I'd be honoured . . .'

The gesture ended by bringing the bottle to his mouth and by taking one long swig, which gurgled and burbled in his throttle. The two of them were making their way down the pathway towards the edge of the quay.

'That's her there now,' the sailor said, and a lump lingered in his throat just long enough to mumble the words he was speaking.

'She's called *The Stars and Stripes*,' N. said, and a lump almost came up into his throat too.

It was hard to say how he thought it was called anything like stars and stripes unless it was part of the same imaginative excitement that brought a lump to his throat. The name on the vessel was largely unreadable. It was only a species of negative presence paying homage to the dark, to the lonely moon which was filling the night on its way among the stars. You couldn't really tell if it was big or small, or new or old, or painted or otherwise. N. tried to eye it more clearly. He couldn't be any more descriptive than to mouth those many *clichés* which he had often used before: it was a form or a shape that you could almost say about it that it was formless and shapeless, apart altogether from that which inhabited the night. But then again, he thought that it couldn't have any real shape or form and called upon another *cliché*: it was a ghost, in the right place, at the right time, in order to instill magic and romanticism as required. Or like an actress, he thought again thinking of another one, an actress draped in black robes on a darkened stage like an unfinished gesture . . .

There was a tiny dapple of golden sunlight left on the horizon where the sun had set. N. wasn't paying attention to anything except what was immediately around him. The water was having a calming effect. In the night it seemed just like another creature, something that could never be imagined during the day. Only a few weak wafts of wind that told you it was there at all. It slapped softly against the quay walls and glugged gently in holes and hollows along the quay. It seemed also to roll along and against the sides of the ship. It wasn't any particular cut or colour, and not even the vague wide expanse out there that was felt before it was seen told you water was there.

But it was there nonetheless, quite distinct and apart from everything else, something unrelated to either street or shop, or to office, stone, or tree, or even to the water of a lake or a river. Man was able to make his own of those earthy things, even the clay itself, he could mould and change them to his own liking. You could say that they were almost part of him, they were loyal to him. But he could do nothing at all with the sea, he had no control over its movement, it was not he who drew its borders and set its contours. The sea was its own boss, a creature apart of and entirely for itself. It was the work of the creator, the work of God. It had its own soul, one that could never be vanquished. If God had his own soul, you could well believe that this was it. Or was it a joint soul, or the entire soul complete? Or how many souls? . . .

N. took another swig of the bottle. He was as taken up with this runaway train of thought as he had been earlier with the burial . . . Did the souls of the world depart into the sea, or were they made by it? Did they go there after they had separated from the body? It stood to reason. The body was laid in the dust and unto dust it did return. The sea was the only thing that never changed, never altered its nature, neither corrupted nor rotted away. And it was restless, skittish, jumpy, just like the mind or the soul itself . . . It is true that there's a lot of pollution in the sea. But still the sea was clean in a way in which neither the earth nor the clay was clean, nor the water on land, nor the whore's eyes yesterday, nor Squimzy's legs, or the twisted tempting lips of the Mystical Body . . .

N. stuck his eyes as sharply as he could through the black band of darkness out into the sea. He wouldn't have been surprised if he had seen Christ walking out there. The sea was the one pure undefiled road that was suitable for his feet . . .

'. . . That's very easy,' the sailor was saying while his gestures descended in a viselike grip on N.'s shoulder. 'Another swig of that bottle, if you don't mind. There's a horde of demons in my gut still screaming for a drink. Don't budge from here. Don't let anyone see you getting on that ship, or getting off either . . . I'll be back and tell you exactly what to do. If it ever happens that they catch you on board — it's highly unlikely, but I'm just telling you anyway, as any Irish American will read you Murphy's law, if anything can go wrong it will — say nothing about me, you never met, saw, or heard anything about me, you know nothing. There are enough of us sailing close to the wind up shit creek. But whatever you do, don't be afraid, and don't get drunk. Maybe you should give me those bottles — the full one anyway. Remember, this is your great adventure, the story of your life . . .'

'The story of my life,' N. said, while he tried to keep separate in his mind the fuzzy shape of Ed's soles from the encompassing darkness as much as he could. N. looked again through the blackness at the water while stitching together the threads of his scattered thoughts. The magic on whose borders he waited made him a bit tipsy just like the booze. It was total magic! It was a mantle of magic which God had thrown upon his creation, that part of his creation he wished to keep hidden. All N. had to do was to take a few steps forward through the jambs of those portals and he would enter that world. There behind him were streets, roads, offices, cemeteries, corpses, coffins, all the usual quotidian junk, the passing jobbery of the dull dead day, the garbage of everyman. Before him lay the ever new fairy cave of wonders, the fantastic phantasmal future, that neither poet nor prophet could properly imagine, was largely unknowable to science, the very frontier of God's own dwelling. N. had turned his back on all that lay behind him. His expectant eyes looked to the challenge of the future, those all too human eyes that were so blind to the mystery that had just come into his life . . .

He was swinging the bottle around in his hand. There was some kind of close relationship between the power of the sea and the power of the bottle, the power of the whiskey. It must have been that it too came from the sea, just as life itself did, as mankind did, if true. It possessed the spark of life as he well knew.

N. let the bottle slide down down into the water, down into the wondrous sea, the hidden sea. He wanted it to be a sign of his past life, and also of the unforeseen life, maybe the liberated life, that was before him. He raised his eyes towards the west, gazed out at that tiny dapple of golden sunlight on the horizon, on the dregs of the day done down . . .

Máirtín Ó Cadhain was born in an Cnocán Glas, Cois Fharraige, Connemara, in 1906. He was educated locally, and a scholarship allowed him to become a National School teacher. On graduating from St. Patrick's College, Drumcondra, Dublin, he returned to Connemara, where he taught in local schools, including Camas and, later, Carnmore. During the Second World War he was interned in the Curragh camp in Kildare for membership in the proscribed Irish Republican Army (IRA). He subsequently became a translator in Dáil Éireann, and Trinity College Dublin appointed him lecturer in Irish in 1956, naming him professor in 1969. He died in 1970. He is best known for his novel *Cré na Cille* (1949), published in the English language by Yale University Press as *Graveyard Clay*, translated by Liam Mac Con Iomaire and Tim Robinson (2016), and *Dirty Dust*, translated by Alan Titley (2015); his short story collections include *Idir Shúgradh agus Dáiríre* (1939), *An Braon Broghach* (1948), *Cois Caoláire* (1953), *An tSraith ar Lár* (1967), *An tSraith Dhá Tógáil* (1970), and *An tSraith Tógtha* (1977). Another novel, *Athnuachan* (1997), and a piece of continuous imaginative prose, *Barbed Wire* (2002), were published posthumously.

Born in Cork in 1947, Alan Titley is a writer and scholar. He is a member of the Royal Irish Academy and Professor Emeritus of Modern Irish in University College Cork, and former head of the Irish Department at St. Patrick's College, Dublin City University. Apart from his scholarly work, he is the author of seven novels, four collections of short stories, numerous plays, one collection of poetry, and several television scripts on literary and historical topics.